CW00524393

It had been twelve years ago, but it had been so unexpectedly strange that I had never forgotten it.

I had almost not become an aviation engineer because of it.

Then, I'd pushed myself to do become one *because* of it. I refused to let something a fortune teller said when I was a teenager stop me from doing what I loved.

The whole experience had been completely ridiculous.

Ava and I had never even talked about it.

She was miffed because she hadn't gotten her fortune done. I would gladly have let her have the experience.

I hated being haunted by those stupid words.

Besides, I'd told myself, it wasn't even possible to meet anyone *beneath* an airplane.

Until it was.

The Lady in the Red Dress

ALSO BY KATHRYN KALEIGH

Contemporary Romance
The Worthington Family

Borrowed Until Monday

The Lady in the Red Dress

On the Edge of Chance

Sealed with a Kiss

Kiss me at Midnight

The Heart Knows

Billionaire's Unexpected Landing

Billionaire's Accidental Girlfriend

Billionaire Fallen Angel

Billionaire's Secret Crush

Billionaire's Barefoot Bride

The Heart of Christmas

The Magic of Christmas

In a One Horse Open Sleigh

A Secret Royal Christmas

An Old-Fashioned Christmas

Second Chance Kisses

Second Chance Secrets

First Time Charm

Three Broken Rules

Second Chance Destiny

Unexpected Vows

Begin Again

Love Again

Falling Again

Just Stay

Just Chance

Just Believe

Just Us

Just Once

Just Happened

Just Maybe

Just Pretend

Just Because

The Lady in the Red Dress

A MODERN CINDERELLA RETELLING

KATHRYN KALEIGH

THE LADY IN THE RED DRESS

ON THE EDGE OF CHANCE PREVIEW

Copyright © 2023 by Kathryn Kaleigh

All rights reserved.

Written by Kathryn Kaleigh.

Published by KST Publishing, Inc., 2023

Cover by Skyhouse24Media

www.kathrynkaleigh.com

No part of this book may be reproduced in any form or by any electronic or mechanical means, including information storage and retrieval systems, without written permission from the author, except for the use of brief quotations in a book review.

This is a work of fiction. Any names, characters, places, or incidents are products of the author's imagination and used in a fictitious manner. Any resemblance to actual people, places, of events is purely coincidental or fictionalized.

To learn more about Kathryn Kaleigh, visit

www.kathrynkaleigh.com

Kathryn Kaleigh

Prologue

Chloé

Twelve Years Ago

"Come on, it'll be fun."

"No," I said, but I knew it was a losing battle.

My cousin Ava had no fear. If there was an adventure to be had, she was going to jump right in with both feet. Her world was danger-free and lovely.

Zydeco music came from all different directions, blending in with what by all rights should have been a discordant messy sound. Instead it was just downright festive.

Ava and I stood in front of a fortune teller's tent with a sign on a stand outside that simply read "Fortunes" in big red letters.

At fourteen years old, Ava and I were dressed identically in white shorts and brand-new light blue t-shirts with *New Orleans* printed across the front. Her long brunette hair was pulled back on top of her head in a ponytail as was my blonde hair. We were as much alike as two best friends could be.

"It's creepy," I said. It was just a regular canopy tent with a white top, but the sides were draped with silk curtains in blues and purples that rippled in the soft breeze coming off the Mississippi River. The door in the front was just an opening created by two panels held back with tasseled rope.

Ava's brows furrowed as she looked at the tent. "It looks cheerful," she said.

"You're weird."

Ava turned and grinned at me. "You love me anyway."

"We should get something to eat," I said, hopefully. Ava was always hungry. "We can get some more beignets."

Ava wrinkled her nose. "We just had those for breakfast."

"Fine," I said. "When my sister comes looking for us and can't find us, you're the one responsible."

"Okay." Ava grinned and dragged me by the elbow toward the tent opening.

I groaned. If Ava weren't my best friend forever, I'd hate her right about now. Even though I didn't know anyone in New Orleans, it was still embarrassing to be seen going into a fortune teller's tent.

As I stepped inside the darkened tent behind her, she held my hand to keep me from going the other way. She knew me too well. The darkness was broken only by the dim light of half a dozen candles on a table at the back of the tent. Sunlight peaked through the curtains, but for the most part, they kept the bright sunlight out.

I wrinkled my nose at the scent of incense. I only knew it was incense because my third grade English teacher used it to keep incense sticks on her desk. She claimed it was calming. Not that anything could keep a classroom full of third graders calm.

Then I saw the young lady sitting on a mat in the middle of the tent. She wore a purple silk scarf over her long black hair. A full skirt spilled out around her.

"Come in," she said. Bells at her wrists jingled as she swept her hands wide. "My name is Marie. I am the great great great granddaughter of Marie Laveau. Sit. I will tell your fortunes."

Marie spoke in a thick accent that sounded a bit like French.

I pushed at Ava to go in front of me, but Ava just pulled me along with her.

We sat down on two pillows on the ground in front of the girl.

"What are your names?"

"I'm Ava and this is Chloé."

I said nothing.

I watched Marie closely. She had glossy red lips and dark eyes framed with dark lashes. One of the most beautiful women I had ever seen, she was about my older sister's age. It didn't matter to me that she was beautiful. I still did not want to be here.

All I had to do was to get it over with and get out of here. Ava could have her fortune read or whatever it was Marie did. I wanted nothing to do with it. The whole thing frightened me.

Marie removed a scarf, revealing a crystal ball sitting in front of her.

"I tell your fortunes," she said.

I was shaking my head. I did not want to know my fortune.

Ava grinned.

"But only one of you," Marie said.

"Why?" Ava asked.

"It's okay," I said quickly. "Do yours."

"Why?" Ava asked again.

"It's what the spirits want." Marie sat back and took her time looking from one of us to the other.

I looked down, not wanting Marie to see me.

Two children screeched as they ran past the tent. I wanted to run with them.

"Do me," Ava said. She was nothing if not a loyal friend. It helped that she really wanted her fortune read.

"No," Marie said. "You."

I slowly lifted my gaze to hers.

Her eyes seemed to glow for just a second. I imagined it. I had to have imagined it.

She smiled slowly at me and held out a hand.

"Give me your hand," she said.

I glanced at Ava, then over my shoulder toward the door.

"Give her your hand," Ava said, impatiently.

I glared at Ava.

"I tell your fortune," Marie said.

Be brave. Be brave.

I placed my palm against Marie's. She closed her eyes.

"We should go," I whispered to Ava. Ava just made a face.

Marie opened her eyes and held her hands above the crystal ball. I put both my hands under my arms, trying hard to ignore the tingling of my palm where she had touched me. My imagination was much too vivid.

Fortune telling is not real.

"I see..." Marie said, stopping and scowling at the crystal ball.

I felt sick to my stomach. This was like one of those ghost stories my mother had on her bookcase. I never should have read any of them.

"You are mechanically inclined," she said.

Ava looked over at me, her eyes wide. "You are."

"I am not."

"She is," Ava said. "She fixed my bicycle."

"The chain had come off," I said, wishing Ava would stop talking. I didn't want anything Marie said to be anywhere near true.

"You will..." Marie stopped again and looked very confused. Or very shocked.

Whatever it was, I just tried to block it out. I forced myself to think about the two new kittens waiting at home for me.

I wanted to be at home. New Orleans frightened me. But my parents wouldn't let my older sister come with her boyfriend unless she brought me and Ava. Sometimes my parents were so clueless.

I had no idea where my sister and her boyfriend were right now. Like having us here was going to make any kind of difference in what they did.

Then Marie looked up into my eyes.

I tried very hard not to squirm. Marie seriously creeped me out. I was terrified of anyone seeing into my future.

"You will meet your soulmate underneath... an airplane."

CHAPTER 1

Chloé

Today

"SERIOUSLY?" I looked at the paperwork request now sitting on my desk. "Today?"

"Yes ma'am. We're out of options."

"Alright," I said with a glance at my Apple watch. I had an appointment with the big boss, Quinn Worthington, in just about two hours.

I could make it.

"I'll be right out," I said, picking the clipboard up and handing it back to Bob. He was one of the top aircraft mechanics at Skye Travels. He'd been here for five years. I'd only worked here for five days and already I knew he was the best. I trusted his judgement.

If he couldn't figure out how to fix something, I wasn't quite sure I could. Nonetheless, it was my job to try.

I closed my office door behind Bob and shrugged off my suit

jacket. Then I took off my silk blouse and hung it carefully in the little closet that was part of my office.

My office. I liked the sound of it. Hated to remind myself that the position was temporary.

My office still had that new building smell. That and coffee. There was always a pot of coffee going in the break room down the hall. It seemed to be a requirement of men. And since I was the only female who worked in this department, well, there was lots of coffee.

I had a big wooden work desk. Not the kind an executive would have, but the kind a girl could spread schematics across. I had a nice lamp and the office chair provided for me was amazing. I never got tired sitting in it.

The office was very clean and very tidy. I kept my desk cleaned off unless I was working on a project. I had two armchairs in one corner with a little table between them. That was for visitors, mostly meetings. Not that I had that many in here. But if I stayed here, I might. That's what today's meeting with Quinn Worthington was about.

At any rate, it was nice to have my own private restroom and closet. Perks of being the maintenance engineer supervisor.

As I changed into shorts and a t-shirt, I contemplated how many people changed clothes at work. Doctors maybe. Firemen?

At any rate, it was something I had to do on occasion, especially days like today.

Dressed now in my fight suit, I sat in one of the armchairs and tied the laces on my work boots.

I pulled my long naturally blonde hair back and, after securing it in a scrunchie, tucked it beneath my cap.

There. A quick glance in the mirror told me that I should be able to take care of the mystery malfunction without coming back smeared with grease. This was not the day to look like I worked in the field.

Another perk of being the engineer supervisor was that one elevator ride took me straight down to the hangar.

A definite perk, I decided as I stepped onto the elevator.

When I reached the bottom floor, a door to the left would take me to the Skye Travels business offices. But I went to the right. To where the good stuff happened.

Downside of being the maintenance engineer supervisor. Spending my days sitting behind a desk.

Any day but today I would be pleased to be getting my hands dirty.

I stopped at a work cabinet on the way out to the hangar and grabbed a pair of work gloves. I'd had my nails done just for today's meeting. But it couldn't be helped.

Bob was waiting for me. He and three technicians stood next to a Phenom 100. It was a brand-new airplane. What could possibly be wrong with it?

Bob handed me the schematic.

"Thank you," I said, taking it from him, but I didn't look at it. I didn't have to. There was nothing about the workings of a Phenom I didn't know. I could work on any airplane, but the Phenom was my specialty.

I crawled beneath the plane so that I could see up into the engine. First, even though I knew they already would have done it, I checked the basics. Nothing wrong there.

A quick glance over my shoulder told me that the men had gone off and left me here.

I shook my head and continued to search for whatever it was that had my men baffled.

It didn't take long before I found it.

One of the gears was missing a pin.

"It's a stripped gear," I said to no one in particular.

"Sounds like a simple fix."

I looked up, nearly bumping my head on the fuselage. A

3

man kneeling also on the other side of the plane was looking at my hands as I checked the lines.

"It is," I said. "But it's damaged the brake line."

He didn't answer right away.

"Can you fix it?"

Balancing with one hand on the concrete, I looked at the man.

First of all I didn't recognize him. Not surprising. I hadn't been here long enough to recognize hardly anyone other than the men I was supervising and I was still learning their names.

Second, he was not one of the mechanics.

He was dressed in a pilot's uniform.

Third, I couldn't see his eyes behind his aviator glasses. For some reason, that always annoyed me. Why couldn't they take off their shades when they were inside the hangar? It wasn't like there was any glaring sunlight inside. The shades merely served to keep what they probably considered a healthy distance between the mechanics and the pilots.

Didn't they realize that there wasn't really all that much difference between us? A pilot had to know how to work on his or her airplane. A mechanic, however, did not have to know how to fly one and rarely did. Still. There was no reason to be snobby about it.

"I can," I said.

"Good," he said with a little nod and a glance at the designer watch on his wrist. "Can you have it ready before Noon?"

"Maybe. I have to check the parts inventory."

He gave me a nod. "I'll check back."

Then he left me to it.

As I stood up and watched him walk away, with that distinctive pilot's swagger, a voice from a very long, long time ago echoed in my head.

You will meet your soulmate underneath... an airplane.

4

I shook my head. And that was exactly why I had never been to a fortune teller since that day when I was fourteen.

They put ridiculous thoughts in a person's head.

Absolutely ridiculous.

CHAPTER 2

Mason Johnson

AFTER LEAVING THE PRIVATE HANGAR, I strolled down the second-floor hallway of Skye Travels to my grandfather's office. The offices were, in a premium position, right off the tarmac.

About a year ago Grandpa had added offices over our private hangar for the airplane maintenance employees including technicians and engineers. Getting the staff in place for that was still a work in progress.

My grandfather Noah Worthington was an impressive man. At nearly seventy years old, he still ran the company he had started—Skye Travels. My Uncle Quinn was the official vice-president, but unofficially he didn't do anything without Grandpa's approval. I figured it was as it should since Grandpa had started the company from a single airplane and made into a successful company. Usually fast growth was hard to manage, but not for Grandpa.

I stopped at the lobby window overlooking the tarmac. All the windows in the building were floor to ceiling glass. Some people had windows to bring the outdoor of the forest inside their homes. Skye Travels had windows to bring the runway and airplanes inside the offices.

I never grew tired of the sound of jet engines outside on the runway or the scent of jet fuel. I'd practically grown up here in the Skye Travels offices, playing at my grandfather's feet while he conducted the business of the most successful private airline company in the country.

While he talked business, expanding Skye Travels into Worthington Enterprises, I played with my collection of toy airplanes and, my favorite, a little toy airport. At the time I hadn't known that many of my so-called toys were collector's items.

But today was my birthday. And Grandpa didn't know I knew what he had gotten me.

I knew because he gave all of his grandchildren something special when they turned thirty. Something they really wanted. And there was nothing I wanted more than the brand-new Phenom 100 sitting out in the hangar. The paint branding it as part of the Skye Travels fleet was still wet, but that didn't make the airplane any less mine.

I was proud to have the red Skye Travels logo splashed across the sides of my plane.

Since today was my birthday, I already had plans for it. I was going to fly it up to Dallas to have drinks with Mindy. Mindy was my Dallas girl. One of the favorites in my proverbial little black book aka my cell phone.

We shared a love for martinis and that was enough for me. I'd take her up in my new plane first, then we'd have a drink, a nice dinner, and a romp in her high rise condo. Maybe we'd fly somewhere for dinner, then back to Dallas for drinks. Either way it would be a good birthday.

Reaching my grandfather's open office door, I automatically knocked.

Grandpa was standing his hands behind his back, looking out the window over the tarmac as he often did. I thought of it as his domain. He had never said that, of course, Grandpa was about as humble as a multi-billionaire could be.

"Come in," he said, looking over his shoulder.

I wasn't a superstitious man, but if I was, I would have known something was wrong in that moment.

He always said. "Come in. Sit with me." Every single time.

But not today.

Not sure what else to do, I went to stand next to him. Matched his stance.

"Today's a big day for you," he said.

"Yes sir."

Grandpa nodded and made a noncommittal sound of agreement. Hopefully agreement.

I had flashbacks to those times when I sat playing at his feet. I knew when Grandpa was working and when I could climb into his lap to show him my latest toy plane. I knew his business voice and his fun Grandpa voice.

Today he was using his business voice.

But I shrugged it off. I was thirty-years-old today. Maybe that was it. Maybe he saw turning thirty as serious business.

I waited, being about as patient as I possibly could be. Patience was not one of my best traits.

"Come sit," he said.

I let out a breath of relief as we went to his sitting area at the corner. Comfy arm chairs. Floor to ceiling windows. Perfect view of the tarmac.

I loved it here. I could sit here all day, watching planes take off and land.

Of course, I liked it better being in the cockpit, but if I was Grandpa's age, I would spend my days watching airplanes.

"I guess you know I have a present for you," he said.

"Yes, sir." I grinned. I couldn't help it.

"Huh. Right."

The silence that followed was unbearable. So I filled it.

8

"The mechanic is repairing the brake line now. There was a missing pin." I didn't tell him that the mechanic was a girl. I kept that to myself along with just how pretty the mechanic's eyes were. Of course I had noticed. I always noticed a pretty girl or any girl for that matter. I couldn't help it. It was my nature.

"Uh huh."

I was practically squirming now. Why was he dragging this out like this?

"I've come to a decision," he said finally.

"What's that?"

Grandpa was not smiling. Not even an ounce of a smile. And when Grandpa gave gifts, he always smiled. Come to think of it, Grandma Savannah should have been here. Getting the gift of an airplane was no small thing.

"You can't have it."

"What?" I sat back, stunned. "Why? It'll be fixed in no time."

"That's not it," Grandpa said.

"Then...?"

"You can have it after you've been married for three months."

My mouth literally fell open.

I had misunderstood. Or it was a joke. Grandpa was messing with me.

I forced a smile. "Good one."

He shook his head. "I'm serious."

He was serious. I could see it in his eyes. Hear it in his voice. I *knew* he was serious. But... I could not understand it.

"No one else had to." I was the oldest of five siblings, but unless I had missed something, seriously missed something, none of my cousins had this kind of stipulation. He'd given some of my cousins high rise condos in his building. Cars and airplanes were not unusual gifts. The airplanes had to stay with Skye Travels, but still...

"I'm trying something new," he said.

No. Not on me. Surely not.

"I don't understand."

"It's not your place to understand," he said. "It's just your place to do it."

"But you can't—"

"I can."

"But who?" Who did he think I was going to marry? I'd never even been engaged. I happily played the field. Always had.

A smile played about Grandpa's lips now. Now he smiled. Not funny.

"Figure it out," he said. "You have plenty to choose from."

"I—"

"And if you even try having one of those fake marriages, the deal is off."

CHAPTER 3
Chloé

THE PROBLEM with the Phenom 100 had been an easy fix. Too easy. I was pretty sure the guys were still testing me.

I didn't mind. I wasn't one of those feminists who got offended when guys didn't think I knew what I was doing.

I knew what I was doing and that was all that mattered.

I just had an affinity for working on airplanes and I liked doing it.

But today, the timing was not the best.

I let Bob know what the problem was. Asked him to have it fixed before Noon.

To his credit, he looked a bit chagrinned and promised to have it fixed within the hour.

With everything under control, I found my way back upstairs to change back out of my flight suit into my business skirt and jacket.

What the men might not realize, or maybe they did, was that today was a very important day for me.

Today I had an interview with Quinn Worthington to make the job I'd had temporarily for five days now into a permanent one.

I'd only heard rumors about why the position was open. It didn't sound like anything serious. The guy had some kind of personal issue and had decided at the last minute not to come back.

So since I was here... I was offered first interview.

Skye Travels was a family business and made no apologies for it. Family owned and operated. They made no excuses for being loyal to family first. And people who worked here became like family.

I actually kind of liked that.

It beat the cold corporate world I had just come from.

Hence, the importance of the interview.

I shook out my hair, ran a quick brush through it, and smeared on some glossy red lipstick. My nails had come out unscathed and I didn't seem to have gotten any grease on me.

It didn't matter that I smelled like jet fuel. Everyone at Skye Travels smelled like jet fuel. The perfume of success.

As I sat at my desk, waiting until time for my meeting/interview, I checked my messages.

I had one text. From my best friend Ava.

> AVA
>
> I have a funny story for you. I'll tell you tonight.

I sent her a quick message back.

> Can't wait.

I didn't have time to start working on any of my projects. I had to head over to the sort of attached corporate building in thirty minutes.

With nothing left to do but wait, I allowed myself to think about the pilot I had just met.

With the bluest blue eyes like a clear summer sky, he was hard not to think about.

A pilot like that was too handsome for his own good.

And I wouldn't go near him.

I wasn't dating anyone right now and I liked it that way. I was enjoying not having any complications in my life.

Honestly, it was the first time since I was sixteen that I hadn't had a boyfriend of some sort and I was enjoying it. I'd never been engaged or anything like that, but working in a man's field brought one of two things. Either men were threatened by me or they wanted to date me.

But I could not get past the one thought that floated about in my brain.

Underneath an airplane.

It had been twelve years ago, but it had been so unexpectedly strange that I had never forgotten it.

I had almost not become an aviation engineer because of it.

Then, I'd pushed myself to do become one *because* of it. I refused to let something a fortune teller said when I was a teenager stop me from doing what I loved.

The whole experience had been completely ridiculous.

Ava and I had never even talked about it.

She was miffed because she hadn't gotten her fortune done. I would gladly have let her have the experience.

I hated being haunted by those stupid words.

Besides, I'd told myself, it wasn't even possible to meet anyone *beneath* an airplane.

Until it was.

CHAPTER 4

Mason

I LEFT my grandfather's office feeling like I'd just come out of a tailspin. Actually I was still in it.

My legs feeling like jelly, I ducked into the first empty room I came to—the conference room down the hall and sat down, keeping my back to the glass wall that bordered the hallway. I didn't want to see anyone right now. I shared an office with my sister, also a pilot. Even though I didn't know if she was in right now or not—she could be on a flight—I did not want to risk seeing her right now.

It was not a good time for me to see anyone.

I didn't want to see anyone or talk to anyone.

It wasn't that I was spoiled. I worked. I'd earned my pilot's license just like everyone else.

I never once felt like the privileged grandson of the company.

All the pilots at Skye Travels were top notch, whether they were family or not. I respected that and I did my part.

I lived in a small apartment. I drove a little BMW, nothing fancy. So what if I liked women. I worked hard and I played hard.

I certainly wasn't the only pilot who had a girlfriend in every port.

I didn't try to hide it and I didn't make excuses for it.

When I got ready to settle down, I would.

Just because I was thirty did not mean I had to be married.

And damn it, today was my birthday. It was supposed to be a happy day. It wasn't every day a guy turned thirty years old.

Grandpa had most definitely rained on my day.

I had to admit it wasn't the airplane so much as it was the marriage part. Grandpa had bought the airplane for me and he would keep it for me. I had little doubt of that. An hour ago I would have said I had no doubt.

Why? Why would he do this? Why would Grandpa pull the rug out from under me like this?

What was so important about being married at age thirty? He said he was trying something new.

It was so unexpected, I didn't know if I wanted to laugh or cry. No. I did know. I definitely wanted to cry.

My phone chimed. A text from Mindy.

MINDY

Happy Birthday Big Guy! What time should I look for you?

Big Guy. I rolled my eyes. I don't know how or why she started calling me that. I was just a regular sized guy. Fit in with the rest of the Worthingtons. We were all just about six feet tall. Dark hair. Clean cut. Boy next door. Once you got to know of the Worthington men, you could pretty much spot the others. Fortunately Houston was big enough that it rarely happened except in those rare occasions we happened to be together at social occasions outside the family.

Grandpa Noah and Grandma Savannah had five children— six if you counted Grandpa's daughter with his first wife. And all his children had children. And now the grandchildren were starting to come. Grandpa had enough grandchildren. It wasn't like he needed me to produce an heir or anything.

I sent Mindy a quick text.

> Something came up. Can't make it.

I took a deep breath. Attempted to examine the sick feeling in the pit of my stomach.

Okay. So Grandpa bought the airplane for me. It wasn't going anywhere.

It wasn't like I was opposed to marriage. My grandparents and parents all had good marriages. Aunts and Uncles, too. Cousins. I'd never had any pressure to settle down.

Maybe that was his deal. Maybe he wanted to see all his grandchildren settled down. He would know that the airplane was a powerful motivator for me. I was a fairly simple man. Didn't take much more than airplanes and women to make me happy.

I opened my phone and scowled as I scrolled through my contacts. I had a category for girls.

Maybe that was little bit pathetic, now that I thought about it.

I had 'um... a lot of girls in here. I went back to the top and went through them again.

Thought about seeing each one of them, one by one, every day for the rest of my life.

There was a reason most all of my girls lived out of town. I couldn't picture spending more than a weekend with a single one of them.

I hesitated, my finger hovering over Christine's name. A pediatrician living in Boston. She was about as close to marriage material as I had in here. But she'd laugh me out of town if I tried to get her to move to Houston, much less to get married.

She'd been married once and had sworn the institution off. I always liked it that she didn't pressure me into more.

That was an important criterion for me in women. I didn't take well to pressure, but truly, what man did?

I closed out of the phone app and stared out across the tarmac. A Skye Travels airplane was coming in. Nice landing. Smooth.

Brought my thoughts back to the Phenom 100. And that brought my thoughts right back around to the mechanic I'd met underneath my airplane.

I'd thought the mechanic was a young man until I saw her face. Then all logical thoughts had flown out of my head. She had perfect bow shaped lips and the green eyes of a siren.

It wasn't like me to be tongue-tied around a girl. It was just that I thought she was a guy. It had thrown me off balance.

Anyway, back to the matter at hand.

In order to get married—the sooner the better—I had to look close to home. Had to find a girl in Houston. I went back to my contacts. Only one girl in my list lived in Houston. She was not an option. I hadn't even talked to her in ages.

I shook my head.

Nope. Not her.

I would just have to find someone local. I had no problem finding women. I went to my dating app of choice.

Surely there was someone on here I could date.

This wasn't my first choice, I preferred to meet women the organic way. Look them in the eye and all that. I was definitely more charming in person than anyone could portray online.

I grinned to myself as I scrolled through the app.

I'd find someone. But... there was a party tomorrow night for my niece's engagement. There were always women at those kinds of things. And there might even be some women I hadn't met yet.

I could do this.

I just had to find someone I liked enough.

CHAPTER 5
Chloé

I'D SAY it had been the easiest interview I'd ever had, but then I remembered that I had already interviewed to get the temporary job. Couldn't say that had been easy.

Quinn Worthington was all business. I liked that. The Worthingtons did a good job of swirling together the professional business aspect with the family owned-business part. Not just anyone could pull that off.

I'd left with not only a job offer that I had accepted on the spot, but also an invitation to a party for one of Quinn's nieces. An engagement party of some sort. He'd called it an invitation, but an invitation from the new employer wasn't really one of those invitations that came with the option of not attending.

Black tie, he said, adding fresh hell to my life.

Since I didn't wear ties, I'd spent some time on the internet figuring out exactly what that meant for me. It meant I needed a formal evening gown.

This called for Ava's help. Ava was my fashion expert guide.

We met at Nordstrom's and after a quick dinner at their restaurant on the third floor, set out to the formal dress area.

"I'm rather surprised that you're going," Ava said as we left the restaurant.

"I don't exactly have a choice."

"I guess not." Ava wrinkled her nose. "You're just really good at finding a way out of things. That's all."

"I am not," I said. I hated when Ava was right about such things.

"Whatever," Ava said. "You need black. Everyone will be wearing black, but there's a reason for that."

"Why?"

Ava looked at me sideways. "Black tie."

"The Internet said—"

"And then you called me. Right?"

I nodded as we entered the dress section. I put a hand on my stomach to try and calm the butterflies. It wasn't the shopping for a dress part. I had no problem with shopping.

It was what the dress represented. It was going outside my comfort zone with a new employer on an occasion I had no experience with.

We'd only been at it for about ten minutes, finding nothing that I really liked, when Ava announced. "I found it."

"Already?" I asked, looking over where she stood flipping through hangers, looking for my size.

"What can I say? You brought the best."

Ava lacked nothing in the confidence zone.

She held up a floor length red silk dress. High neck. Long sleeves. High low front.

"It's red," I said. "You said it needs to be black."

"I changed my mind," she said. "It's red, but it's elegant. It's you."

I ran my fingers along the silky material.

"Really?" I asked, with a glimmer of hope. "It's so... plain." It was nothing like what I had expected Ava to pick out.

Nothing like what I had imagined. I had imaged a low-cut bodice with a high slit up the side.

"Look," she said, "It has this cute sequined band at the waist that dresses it up. At least try it on. And it's full, like you like."

"Okay," I said. I was cautiously optimistic that it would look as good on me as it did on the hanger.

"Look," she said. "It has a pocket for your phone."

I laughed at Ava's enthusiasm.

If this dress fit like it was supposed to, it would be perfect.

And it was perfect.

It took us longer to find shoes than it did to buy the dress.

CHAPTER 6
Mason

AFTER VALETING MY CAR, I walked through the doors, held open by a formally dressed doorman, of the luxury hotel and headed to the bank of elevators that would take me to the designated party area on the third floor.

I'd been here before, but this was the first time I could remember coming alone.

I had decided after much consideration that if I was going to find a wife, it would not be prudent to have a girl on my arm, so to speak.

Sometimes bringing a date worked with meeting other women—most women find a man more attractive if he was already vetted by another, but I had a feeling that tactic might not work with finding a wife.

I checked my profile as I waited for the elevator. I'd changed up my profile a bit. Added in there that I was looking for a wife.

So far no one had responded.

The elevator opened and I stepped inside, sliding my phone in my pocket. The lack of responses on my dating app left me feeling a bit deflated.

It might be harder to find a wife than I had expected.

It would have been nice if Grandpa had given me some kind of warning about this stipulation ahead of time. But after giving it some thought, I realized that I actually liked a challenge.

Stepping off the elevator, I saw that I was a little bit early. I spotted my cousin Dylan Worthington across the way and headed in his direction.

"How's it going?" I asked.

"Going okay," he said, looking over my shoulder. "Where's your date?"

"I don't have one."

Dylan looked at me with a vague expression of disbelief. "Are you feeling okay?" he asked.

"I guess so."

I hadn't considered whether or not I should tell anyone else about my quest to find a wife, but Grandpa hadn't said anything about it being a secret.

"I need a wife," I said, sticking my hands in my pockets and looking around the room to see if I might spot one.

Dylan stared at me a moment.

"Don't tell people that," he said.

"Why not?"

"Because they'll know you're an idiot."

I faced Dylan and looked him squarely in the eye. "It seems like the best way to rule out women who don't want to get married."

Dylan was shaking his head in disbelief. "Have you thought about how many women it will attract?" He kept his voice low. "Women who will be after you for the wrong reasons."

"Gold diggers," I said with a little nod.

Dylan sighed. "Please don't tell people."

"Seemed like a good idea to speed things up."

"Right," Dylan said. "The Phenom."

"Exactly," I said, thinking he finally understood the urgency of the situation.

"You're an idiot," Dylan said.

I wasn't above a good fistfight, but this wasn't the time or place.

Besides, now that he pointed it out, I acknowledged to myself that he was probably right. I just would not tell Dylan that I'd put it on my dating profile.

"I'll find somebody," I said.

Dylan was still looking at me like I was an idiot.

"It's not that easy," he said.

I grinned. "You made it look easy." I distinctly remembered attending his wedding.

"You know," he said. "for someone who has so much experience with women, you don't know much about relationships, do you?"

I made a face at him and turned around. There really wasn't much I could say.

Unfortunately, my cousin was right.

Dylan's wife Zoe walked up.

"Hey Mason."

"Hi Zoe."

She looked over my shoulder. "Where's your date?"

Looking over at Dylan, I shook my head.

"What?" Zoe asked.

"Mason didn't bring a date. He's here to find a wife."

Zoe's eyes widened. "Oh. My. God."

I scowled at Zoe. Seriously? From the reaction I was getting from my cousin and his wife, maybe my grandfather had a good point.

Maybe I really did need to change my ways.

24

CHAPTER 7
Chloé

At Ava's insistence, I took an Uber to the party. I hadn't understood why she was so adamant about that until we pulled up at the hotel.

I had what I considered to be a serviceable Jeep. It was only two years old and was nice enough, but it would have stood out like a sore thumb among the luxury cars people were pulling up to the hotel in and having valeted, not to mention the limousines.

Ava had helped me get ready, all the way down to getting into the car, but she wouldn't come with me. She couldn't, of course, since she wasn't invited, but it didn't keep me from asking. About ten times.

On the drive over, I had felt overdressed and out of place. I'd been worried that I would be the only one wearing a formal. This was exactly the same reason I did not dress up for Halloween. I had a pathological fear of dressing up as something silly and being the only person in a costume.

But when I got there and saw other women going inside the hotel, I blew out the breath I had been holding. I was most certainly not overdressed.

My dress was perfect.

I'd let Ava work on my hair. She'd pulled it up into what she called a messy-do, leaving just enough strands down to frame my face. She'd done my makeup, too. I wasn't opposed to dressing up and wearing makeup, I just didn't have very many occasions to do so.

A valet opened my car door and held out a hand to help me out of the car.

I felt a little bit like a princess as I walked through the door held open by another valet.

A third man—the concierge, also dressed in a black formal suit greeted me just inside the doors.

"Good evening, Miss. Are you here for the Worthington party?"

"Yes," I said, although I hadn't thought about it being a Worthington party, exactly.

"It's on the third floor," he said. "May I escort you there?"

"Yes," I said. Was this customary? Maybe it was just that I worked around men all the time who treated me like one of the guys. I had almost forgotten what it was like to dress up and be treated like a lady.

It was probably a good reason to think about maybe dating again. I brushed off the thought as soon as it passed through my head. I was just starting a new job and I would be putting everything into it. Not only that, but also I was living in a new city, getting to know it. Houston was a lot different from Pittsburgh where I had spent most of my adult life.

After I thanked the concierge and stepped off the elevator, I realized I was fashionably late. Ava and I had spent a little too much time getting me dressed and then the traffic had been back-to-back on Westheimer near the Galleria. Another one of the things I had to learn. Traffic patterns in different areas.

The room was elegantly decorated with little standing tables covering with white table cloths scattered around the room, leaving plenty of room for people to mingle. There was only one sitting area and there didn't appear to be any room left there at the moment.

The servers wore white suits and walked around carrying trays of champagne.

Dozens of women, most dressed in black, just as Ava had predicted and men, almost all dressed in black or charcoal suits. There were some groups of women standing together and some men standing together, but most people seemed to be paired off.

My discomfort returned in an instant. I was here alone with people I didn't know. Maybe I was supposed to have brought a date.

It was Quinn Worthington, the only person I recognized, who came to my rescue.

"I'm so glad you could make it," he said. "There are several people to introduce you to."

Quinn turned to scan the crowd for some of those people and when he did, I saw *him* across the room.

The man—the pilot—I had met underneath the airplane stood across the room and he was looking right at me.

"There's my wife," he said. "Come. Meet Noelle."

I followed Quinn as he deftly wove through the crowd but out of the corner of my eye, I watched the pilot watch me. His gaze followed me until we were swallowed into the folds of exquisitely dressed beautiful people.

His wife, Noelle was one of those.

"Lovely dress," she said. "I started to wear my red dress."

I immediately liked her. She was accepting and seemed genuinely friendly.

CHAPTER 8
Mason

"MASON."

I heard someone calling my name.

Dylan. Then Zoe. Then Dylan again. But it took a minute for it to register with me as I watched the girl wearing red follow my uncle through the crowd. I watched until they stopped and Uncle Quinn introduced her to Aunt Noelle.

"Mason. Are you sure you're okay?"

I pulled my gaze away from the girl in the red dress with beautiful blonde hair somehow secured in what looked like a messy up-do, but at the same time, made her the most beautiful girl at the party.

"Yes," I said, distractedly. "Do you know who that girl is?" I asked.

"Which girl?" Dylan asked.

I nodded toward the girl. "The one with Uncle Quinn. The one in the red dress."

"No," he said.

"I don't know either," Zoe said. "She obviously knows Dylan's dad."

"Everyone does," I said, mostly to myself.

Everyone should know Uncle Quinn. He was, after all, the CEO of Skye Travels.

She looked a little nervous. I could tell even from here. But that smile... that smile struck me in the heart like Cupid's arrow.

"I'm going to marry her," I said.

"You haven't even met her," Zoe said.

"He's determined to find a wife," Dylan pointed out.

"So you say," she said. "I don't think it works that way."

"It does for me," I said, setting my untouched champagne glass on the tray of a server walking past.

With my jaw set in determination, I navigated toward Uncle Quinn and the girl in red.

When I stood two feet from her, she turned and looked at me.

I saw recognition in her lovely green eyes.

How could she possibly recognize me? She and I had never met.

Maybe she felt the same thing I felt. Maybe it was fate.

Our gazes locked and I, too, had the sense that I had seen her before.

But at the same time I was certain we had not met.

Uncle Quinn seemed to notice me then.

"Chloé," he said. "this is Mason. My nephew."

Chloé. So that was her name. The beautiful woman in red.

She didn't say anything. She just looked at me.

I'm not sure if she stepped in my direction or if I moved closer to her, or both, but either way, Uncle Quinn and Aunt Zoe faded into the background.

"It's a little crowded," I said.

"A little."

"Walk with me? For a glass of champagne and a breath of fresh air on the balcony."

With a glance over her shoulder at Uncle Quinn who was talking to Aunt Zoe and seemed to have forgotten that either one of us was there, she took the hand I offered. I zigzagged a path through the crowd taking us to the balcony.

Just before we stepped outside, I remembered that I had offered her champagne. I reluctantly released her hand to snag two glasses from a passing server and handed one to her.

The nighttime breeze was soft and filled with the scent of magnolia blossoms.

Out here on the balcony, the music from the little three-man orchestra wasn't nearly so loud, nor were the voices. The quiet was deafening.

I led her to the balcony railing overlooking a little park below filled with twinkling lights where I had stood many times with many different women.

But with Chloé standing next to me, I felt as though I was seeing it for the first time.

CHAPTER 9
Chloé

WITH MASON firmly holding my hand, I allowed him to lead me through a set of French doors out onto a balcony over-looking a park of some sort away from the city streets.

It much quieter out here and the wind carried the fresh scent of flowers.

There was another couple standing, their heads bent together at the other end of the balcony.

My heart was pounding at a dangerous rate.

Mason was the same pilot I had met in the hangar early. The man I had met *underneath the Phenom 100*. And yet he didn't seem to recognize me. But how could he? I did not look in any way like the same person.

I had been wearing a formless flight suit, my hair tucked beneath a cap, and no makeup.

Now was dressed in a formal red gown, my hair pulled up on top of my head, and red lipstick.

I knew I looked like a completely different person and on top of that, we were in a completely different setting.

It did not seem prudent to tell him that we had already, sort of, met, at least not at this particular moment.

"You're not from here," Mason said.

"How do you know that?" I asked, looking into his blue eyes that seemed deeper than the deepest ocean.

"It's just a guess," he said. "I haven't seen you at one of these things."

"You're right," I said. "I'm from Pittsburgh."

"What brings you to Houston?"

"Work," I said, bringing the glass of champagne to my lips. It was in that moment, that I decided to keep what I did to myself. Just for the moment, I wanted to be someone else.

I did not want to be Chloé, the flight engineer or even Chloé, the supervisor.

I just wanted to be Chloé, the girl in the red dress who had captured the interest of a handsome pilot.

It would only be fleeting. I knew pilots well enough to know that. I'd only met a couple who didn't like to play the field. Guys with pages and pages of girls in their little black books.

This guy, Mason, was too handsome to be any different. But that was okay. Tonight I could be someone else. At least for as long as no one like Quinn pointed out that I wasn't actually part of this group, but that I worked for Skye Travels. An employee.

"Are you just visiting, then?" he asked.

I shook my head. "Probably not."

He grinned. It was a sexy grin. One of those heart-melting grins that would be hard for any girl to resist.

"Good," he said simply.

The other couple who had been standing outside went back inside.

"Dance with me," he said.

"Dance?" I shook my head. "No one is dancing."

"No? Well, they should be."

As I looked back toward the doors back inside, I was reminded that this was a work function for me.

"I don't think it's kind of party."

32

"Then why have such beautiful music?"

"I don't know," I said.

Before I knew what he was doing, he took the champagne flute from my hands and set it on the railing.

I did not know how to waltz. But with Mason, I soon discovered, it wasn't necessary to know. All I had to do was hold onto him and follow.

He placed a hand on the small of my back and twirled me around the balcony.

He kept his eyes on mine, a little smile playing about his lips.

"Are you always this reckless?" I asked, my voice coming out sounding breathy to my own ears.

"Am I being reckless?" he asked, leaning forward to whisper in my ear.

Oh yes. "Maybe a little." A lot. But I didn't want him to stop. My heart was spinning out of control even as he spun me around the balcony.

He was so very charming. And the word handsome didn't do him justice.

As we danced, I wondered why he was alone. Maybe he wasn't alone.

"What troubles you Mon chéri?"

"Nothing," I said, quickly. I couldn't tell him. I couldn't tell him that I was worried that he had a girl waiting inside for him.

Not when he was using French words of endearment. But I had to tell him something.

"I don't want to keep you from your obligations," I said.

"I don't have obligations tonight," he said. "It's a party."

I smiled and bit my bottom lip. I had to look down to keep my heart out of my eyes.

I reminded myself that this was not real.

This was just one night.

One night to be someone else.

CHAPTER 10
Mason

THE EVENING AIR was heavy with the scent of magnolias. The soft music drifted outside, just low enough that I could hear Chloé's breath. Minty. She smelled like flowers and mint. And... I detected the faint scent of jet fuel. That's what happened when a guy spent his days at the airport. The scent of jet fuel seemed to be everywhere even when it wasn't.

Maybe I just imagined all of it, but it didn't matter.

I was enchanted by Chloé.

It didn't take me more than a split second to discover that Chloé did not know how to waltz. She stepped on my feet a couple of times and had some trouble following me, but she was a trouper. She did a good enough job of keeping up. She could have stepped all over my feet and I wouldn't have cared.

When I looked at her, I felt a magic between us.

Something I couldn't explain.

I didn't know her, but I didn't have to know her.

Taking her hand, I pulled her back to the railing and handed her one of the glasses of wine.

She took a minute to catch her breath. Then placed her lips against the rim to drink and closed her eyes.

With the moonlight reflecting on her hair and the soft music surrounding us, I imagined kissing her.

Normally, in what I was beginning to think of as my old days —which was actually just last weekend—I would have simply pulled her to me and kissed her.

But not Chloé. That wasn't how a man treated the woman he was going to marry.

I didn't quite have a handle on how that was supposed to go, but I felt confident that I would figure it out.

My phone chirped, telling me I had a dating app alert.

Chloé slowly lowered her glass and looked at me with an odd expression.

I reached into my pocket to put it on silent, but before I could, it chirped again.

Knowing I looked more than a little guilty, I put it on silent and stuffed it back into my pocket.

Maybe it took some time for my profile to update. And Dylan was probably right. I'd probably have all sorts of women answering my ad for a wife. But now I didn't need them. Now I could delete the app.

"Do you need to answer that?" she asked.

"What? No." Maybe she didn't recognize the distinctive chirping sound. I sought to distract her.

"The moon is lovely tonight."

She followed my gaze. "Yes. It is. I think it's supposed to rain tonight, though."

"Is it?" I normally kept up with the weather. All pilots did.

"Yes," she said. "It's a small chance and by tomorrow morning, it will be clear."

I grinned at her. She truly was the perfect woman for me. Like me, she watched the weather. Most of my dates got annoyed with my obsession with the weather.

And either she didn't recognize the dating app chirp or she was easily distracted. Either way, it was my good fortune.

I would be deleting the thing before the night was over.

"Are you hungry?" I asked.

"A little."

"Wait here," I said. "I'll go find us something to eat."

When she smiled at me, I almost didn't go. I almost didn't leave her.

But since I couldn't kiss her yet, the least I could do was to feed her.

"I'll be right back," I said, kissing the back of her fingers before I left. "Don't go anywhere."

CHAPTER 11
Chloé

WILD HORSES COULDN'T PULL me away from Mason. Not tonight.

Maybe tomorrow.

He'd had me dancing on the balcony, for God's sake. Anyone could have walked out and saw us. In fact, anyone could have seen us through the windows. But I didn't care.

I sort of liked it that people could see us.

I liked it that for one night, just one night, my date was a handsome pilot. The kind of man I never dared to date. I'd dated a meteorologist and I'd dated a college professor. I tried to keep work and dating as separate as possible.

My dress was perfect. The night was perfect.

I wasn't wearing my watch, but I had my phone tucked in the pocket of my dress. When I pulled it out to check the time, I saw that had a message.

Several messages.

From work. From the hangar.

WORK

Sorry to bother you. We can't reach Bob.

> We have a plane that needs to go out tonight.
> Sort of an emergency. Having a malfunction.

> Can you possibly come out? See if you can
> fix it?

What was wrong with the men? Feeling more annoyed than I probably should, I texted back.

> I'm in the middle of something. Can it wait?

> The passenger needs to fly out tonight. If we
> can't get the plane fixed, we have to buy him
> a commercial ticket.

I pressed my fingers against my brow. If they were messing with me, I was going to fire every one of them.

Pacing to the door, I saw Mason talking to a pretty brunette in a black gown. I should have worn black, I thought.

Maybe wearing red sent the wrong message.

Maybe Mason had forgotten that I was waiting for him.

Maybe a lot of things, but I had a job to do. As supervisor, I was on call as needed. This was one of those as needed times, apparently. I sighed.

> I'll be there within the hour.

I wasn't sure just how far away the airport was from here, but I was pretty sure I could be there from most anywhere in Houston in less than an hour.

I watched Mason for a few more minutes.

My plan to have just one night with him had already come to an end and I knew it.

Maybe I should tell him I had to leave.

I watched the brunette reach out and adjust his tie.

No. I didn't need to tell him where I was going. But I did

need to tell Quinn. Quinn was the one who had asked me here. He was the one who needed to know that I was leaving for work.

I checked my phone one more time. Just to make sure that the men hadn't figured it out. To make sure they didn't need me after all.

But no such luck.

We'll see you then. Thank you.

By the time I stepped back through the doors, I didn't see Mason anywhere. Fortunately Quinn was easy enough to find.

And just like that, my magical evening, my one chance to be someone else for even just a few minutes, perchance a few hours, had come to an abrupt end.

CHAPTER 12
Mason

After stepping back inside, my sister, Brooklyn, immediately intercepted me.

"Please tell me I heard wrong," she said, her voice clear over the voices and music that had been pleasant background noise when I was outside on the balcony.

"About what?" I knew perfectly well what she was talking about, but I wouldn't give her the satisfaction.

"You know what," she said, scowling at me. "What have you been doing? Your tie is crooked."

I looked down. "No it's not."

"It is." She reached up to straighten it. "There. Now it's straight."

I took a step around her.

"Where are you going?"

"To get food," I said. "I'll talk to you later."

"Where did you leave your date?" she asked.

"I don't have—" Ah. But I did. "On the balcony," I said, then immediately regretted the words. "Don't bother her."

Brooklyn gave me one of her innocent I-would-never-do-that looks.

"We'll talk later," she said as I stepped around her.

Hurrying now, I filled a tray with all sorts of food, from little crab cakes to blueberry tarts, since I didn't know what Chloé liked.

I added two fresh glasses of champagne to my tray, even though I hadn't touched my other one, and took it all with me back toward the balcony. I ignored the funny looks I got.

But when I reached the doors and stepped out onto the balcony, holding my food laden tray, Chloé was not there. Two other couples had come out to enjoy the night air. One, on the far end, was making out and really needed to get a room.

Two weeks ago, that could have been me. but I was a changed man now. A man on the mission of taking a wife.

Going back inside, I set the tray on the nearest table and stood, hands on my hips, looking around the room. It shouldn't be hard to spot a pretty blonde in a red dress in a room of ladies wearing black.

Deciding she must have gone to the restroom, I milled about in that direction, waiting.

After about ten minutes, when she didn't come out, I went in search of Uncle Quinn.

"The girl you introduced me to," I said. "Chloé. Have you seen her?"

"Yes," Uncle Quinn said. "She had to leave."

"Quinn," Zoe interrupted. "Can I borrow you for a moment?"

"Of course," Uncle Quinn said. "Can you excuse me?"

Realizing that Uncle Quinn wasn't going to be any help whatsoever, I decided to go downstairs. See if the concierge had seen her.

"Jonathan," I said, recognizing the man behind the desk. "There was a girl named Chloé. You didn't happen to see her leave did you?"

"There was a young lady in a red dress. I didn't catch her name though."

"She left?"

"Yes sir. I believe she took an Uber."

"An Uber." I stood there, looking out the door toward the street.

My lady in red had fled and I had no way of knowing how to find her.

CHAPTER 13
Chloé

THE RESTAURANT/BAR across the freeway from the Skye Travels airport terminal was crowded, as expected, for a Saturday night. During the week, it was frequented mostly with pilots and other airport staff, but on weekends it attracted people completely unrelated to the airport.

I sat in a booth at the back across from Ava.

Music from an old-fashioned juke box played eighties music that went straight to my heart, and normally would have filled me with happiness. Usually. Tonight I wasn't feeling particularly happy, with or without eighties music.

"Tell me what happened," Ava said, picking up her pretty pink cosmopolitan and taking a sip. "And don't leave out any detail."

I sipped my martini, hiding my discomfort behind it.

Last night wasn't anything I wanted to share with anyone, not even Ava. But she had a way of getting me to talk about everything... just about everything.

"It was nice," I said. "But I had to leave early."

Ava set her glass down. "Wait. How early?"

"I don't know. I was there maybe an hour," I said, then lowered my voice and added. "At most."

"Wait a minute." Ava said, aghast. "All that. That dress. And you only stayed for one hour?"

"Work," I said with a shrug.

Ava rolled her eyes, then closed them for a moment. When she opened them and looked at me again, she just shook her head. "What am I going to do with you?"

"I couldn't help it," I said. "There was an airplane malfunction at the hangar."

"So you left the party to go work on an airplane."

I shrugged and took another sip of my drink.

"Please," Ava said. "Please tell me you at least talked to someone."

"I did."

"You did?" Ava looked hopeful. "Then at least people knew you were there?"

"A couple of people," I said. "I didn't really know anyone other than my boss. I met his wife." A smile crossed my lips, even as I tried not to smile. "And their nephew."

Ava had glanced away, toward the front door, but at my words, she jerked her gaze back to mine.

I slid an olive off a toothpick with my teeth and looked at her with a raised eyebrow.

"Tell me more about this nephew," Ava said.

I glanced around, but didn't recognize anyone.

"His name is Mason."

"Mason. What is his last name?"

"I don't know."

"If he's Quinn Worthington's nephew, then he must be related to the family."

"Oh. Good point," I said. "And he's a pilot."

"He is not," she said.

"He is."

"Chloé." Ava shoved her drink aside and leaned forward. "You don't date pilots."

"I'm not dating him."

With a quick nod of her head, Chloé sat back. "Right."

Then her cell phone chirped.

Chirped.

"What's that?" I asked.

"What's what?"

"That sound on your phone. What is it?" I knew I'd heard that sound before.

"It's my dating app." She pulled out her phone and held it up for me to see. I recognized the app, but I had never used it.

My heart sank, taking my newfound hopes and dreams with it.

"Mason uses that app," I said, sitting back in the booth.

"Seriously?" she asked. "He's on here?"

I shrugged, trying to pretend it didn't matter.

"That's great," she said.

What could possibly be good about Mason being on a dating app?

"Let's look him up and see what he's up to," she said, with a gleeful expression.

Maybe Ava wasn't so crazy after all.

CHAPTER 14
Mason

IT WAS NOT my usual Saturday night scene. Instead of going out, looking for someone to spend some quality time with, I drove up to my grandparents' house. It had been awhile since I had visited Grandpa Noah and Grandma Savannah at home. He'd probably think I was trying to suck up to him about the airplane, but truly I wasn't.

They had a big house off of Memorial Drive with a gated private driveway. I punched in the code and drove over the bricked driveway to park near the front door.

Their lawn, as always, was perfectly landscaped. As far as I knew, Grandma Savannah still did the flowers herself. The scent of magnolia blooms filled the air along with roses and other flowers I didn't recognize.

Grandpa Noah answered the door.

"Mason," he said. "Is everything alright?"

A sure sign that I hadn't been to visit in far too long.

"Everything's fine," I said, handing him a bottle of his favorite cabernet.

"Where's your date?" he asked, looking past me. "Bring her in."

"I didn't bring her," I said as I followed Grandpa inside. "Is Grandma Savannah here?"

"She's in her office, working on a project." He stopped and looked at me. "You need to talk to her?"

Grandma Savannah was a psychologist, a well-known good one. She might be nearly seventy years old, but she showed no signs of slowing down. In fact, if she was still working on projects, she must be going as strong as ever.

"Not necessarily," I said. "I just had some time and thought I would come by to visit."

Grandpa looked at me sideways. "Well, come on in. We'll open this wine and try it out."

No matter how many times someone brought him this wine or any wine for that matter, he always said the same thing. *We'll try it out.*

We went into the living room, where it looked like he'd been reading.

"I didn't mean to disturb you," I said.

"Nonsense," he said. "I'm always happy to see any one of you."

By any one of us, I knew he meant my siblings and cousins, and, of course, his children.

"Reading anything good?" I asked as he took the wine over to the cabinet to grab a corkscrew.

"Just a murder mystery," he said, deftly pulling the cork loose.

I picked up the book. Looked at the cover. "Looks like a romance."

"Really?" Grandpa said. "I didn't notice."

He kept a straight face as he handed me a glass of wine and sat across from me.

I took a sip of the wine, considering the possibility that Grandpa Noah, founder and owner of the most successful private airplane company in the country read romance novels.

KATHRYN KALEIGH

He and Grandma had a romantic story of second chances. And they were as happy as any two people could be. I decided it fit him just fine.

"Let me know if I should read it when you finish," I said.

"I can already recommend it. The author has a whole series if you want to get into the habit of reading."

I wondered briefly how he knew I wasn't reading lately, but since he knew everything, I couldn't possibly be surprised.

"I'll check it out," I said. But I knew I wouldn't. At least not right now. I was too absorbed in a romance of my own.

"Why aren't you on a date?" Grandpa asked. "It's Saturday night."

I took a sip of the wine. "You might remember," I said. "You put me on a mission to find a wife."

Grandpa held his glass balanced on one knee. "Can't find a wife sitting here with me," he said.

I waved a hand in dismissal. "I already found one."

Grandpa tried not to smile. I could tell by the way the corners of his mouth turned up at both corners. He sipped his wine to hide his amusement.

"Where is she?" he asked.

"That's the problem," I said. "I don't know."

Grandpa studied me. "Explain."

So I did. I told him about the lady in red and how she was the one I was going to marry.

Except that she had vanished before I could find out who she was.

"I had a similar problem with your grandmother," Grandpa Noah said. "Maybe I can help you."

CHAPTER 15
Chloé

Ava scooted over to my side of the booth and together we began scrolling through her dating app.

"Tell me if you think you see him," she said. "He could be using a fake name."

"Don't worry." I wasn't angry. Not exactly anyway. I had no right to be angry. I'd just met the guy. He had no obligation to not use a dating app if he wanted to.

Ava used a dating app and I'd seen her keep her profile up while she was actually dating someone. She might not check it, but she kept it.

But I was disappointed. I figured it was okay to be disappointed. Just because he was my just-one-night-fantasy-date did not mean that I was his.

And even if I was, he couldn't have predicted that he would meet me.

It just happened that I didn't use dating apps.

We scrolled through all sorts of guys. Most of the guys who got past Ava's filters were conservative professionals. Mason could easily be in there.

The thought of her accidentally going out with Mason

chilled my blood. I had no problem finding guys to date when I wanted to, but Ava was a girly girl and she was proficient at flirting. Skills she was always trying to teach me.

"Wait," I said. "Go back."

I studied the photo of Mason wearing aviator shades.

"That's him," I said, rolling my eyes.

"I thought—" Ava stopped. "Right. The shades." She took a screen shot and zoomed in. "I bet he has nice eyes."

"Gorgeous blue eyes," I said.

"Don't hate him for wearing shades," she said. "I would have skipped past him."

"I don't. What does it say?" I asked.

"Let's see." Ava scrolled through his profile, reading intently. I concentrated on sliding my last olive from the toothpick. Sometimes I think I only ordered martinis to get the olives.

"Basic stuff," Ava said. "He lives in Houston. He's a pilot."

"We already knew that."

Ava nodded and kept reading.

Then she suddenly closed her phone and set it face down on the table.

"What are you doing?" I asked.

"Nothing."

"Not nothing." I went to pick up her phone, but she slid it away. "Tell me," I said. "Whatever it is, it can't be all that bad."

Ava's eyes widened. "Oh, but it is. It's very bad."

She slid off my side of the booth back to hers.

I looked at her through narrowed eyes, trying to think of what could possibly be so terrible that she didn't want to tell me.

"What?" Then I realized what it had to be. "He doesn't like girls?"

"Oh. He likes girls all right."

I kicked Ava under the table.

"Ow. Okay." She unlocked her phone. "You have to see it for yourself."

"I'm not sure I want to," I said as she slid the phone over to me, with Mason's profile open.

"Just read it."

I reminded myself that it didn't matter.

I don't date pilots anyway.

And I had just been looking for one night of escapism.

I had not been looking for a long-term relationship with a man I'd met underneath an airplane, of all things. And then he didn't even recognize me.

Sufficiently worked into a state of not caring, I read the part of the profile that Ava wanted me to see.

After I read it, I looked up at her. "You're right. It's very bad."

She nodded solemnly.

"He's not very smart, is he?" she asked.

I nodded, then shook my head.

It was hard to defend a guy who was obviously lacking in discretion.

I looked back down and read it again. Maybe I had been mistaken. But there it was in black and white.

I am looking for a wife.

CHAPTER 16

Mason

I HAD a Monday morning flight out to Denver. A flight that was going to keep me there for at least a couple of days.

That was going to give me some time on my hands.

It also gave me several hours to think. Like most other pilots I knew did, I did my best thinking in the cockpit.

No distractions. No one to talk to. No Internet. Besides, it was a beautiful day to be in the air. Clear blue sky. White wispy clouds here and there. Sunlight at my back.

The little Cessna airplane was pleasantly familiar and after we were in the air, the flight path steady, I allowed myself to replay Friday night's party.

I still didn't know why Chloé had left or where she had gone.

I hadn't been gone *that* long. Just long enough to get a tray of food. Other than being stopped by my sister, no one had intercepted me.

There was no obvious reason why she would have disappeared on me.

I hadn't said anything to her about getting married. Even if I had, girls liked that sort of thing. Didn't they?

I checked my computer gauges. Made some minor adjustments. Flying into the mountains was a bit trickier than flying over the flat lands of Texas. More turbulence, too, so we had to keep our seatbelts fastened. Not that my passenger cared one way or the other.

My passenger, Benjamin Gray, was a quiet man who spent the whole trip typing away on his computer, hardly saying a word. The only thing he ever asked for was bottled water. Very low maintenance.

We typically provided our passengers with drinks and snacks of their choice. They had to tell us far enough in advance, but it usually wasn't a problem.

Benjamin had flown with me several times and I knew no more about him now than I did after our first flight.

"Prepare for landing," I said, my words running together into one word, into the speaker. A courtesy statement. Everyone knew when the airplane started to drop altitude, we were going in for a landing.

The shop had been closed this morning when I got to the airport, so I hadn't had the opportunity to check on the status on the Phenom repairs. Not that I was allowed to take the plane right now even if it was repaired.

Grandpa might let me take it up for a spin. He wasn't heartless. Besides, a plane was meant to be flown. I could justify anything.

Thinking about the Phenom circled my thoughts back around to the girl who had been working on those repairs.

I usually knew who worked at Skye Travels, but somehow I had missed this girl.

It was just as well, I thought, that I hadn't known about her and I had no reason to be thinking about her. I had already picked out the girl I was going to marry

But there had been something about her lovely green eyes that I couldn't stop thinking about.

I lowered the landing gear.

This marriage thing might be harder than I expected.

If I was already having trouble keeping my thoughts on just one girl, it was not a good sign that I would be able to keep my thoughts on one girl for the rest of my life.

Well, I thought, I wasn't married yet.

I couldn't help it if female engineers were particularly sexy, maybe partly because of their rarity.

If I wanted to think about the pretty green-eyed girl who knew how to work on airplanes and wasn't afraid to do so, then there was no one who would say I couldn't.

I had to accept that there was a faint—more than a faint—possibility that I might not ever see Chloé again.

I would, however, talk to Uncle Quinn again before I gave up on her. Surely he knew more than just her name.

In the event that I couldn't find Chloé, maybe I'd have a conversation with the airplane engineer. Find out if we had a connection.

The problem with this whole thing was that I had only met airplane girl for a few seconds and I knew in my heart of hearts that she and I did have some kind of connection. It might be nothing more than a love of airplanes, but there was something there, no doubt.

I had good instincts on these kinds of things.

CHAPTER 17
Chloé

MY FIRST WEEK as official supervisor was busy. I hardly had time to do more than look up from the paperwork that got thrown onto my desk.

I'd been warned that there would be some paperwork, but I'd expected blueprints, not inventories and work schedules for the men. It was my job to make sure we had all the parts we needed and that the men were here to use them.

The men didn't bother me so much. They seemed to have gotten past whatever tests they had been giving me. Either that or they were too busy to look up.

They probably got tired of me fixing everything they threw at me anyway. Not much fun to haze someone who wasn't easy to ruffle.

The weather was still cool enough that we kept the doors to the hangar open. I didn't have much experience with the scorching Texas heat, but I heard enough talk about it to have a bit of trepidation about it.

My office had a window that overlooked the hangar and when those doors were open, I had a decent view of the runways.

I caught myself watching the airplanes and thinking about

Mason when I surfaced from the mounds of paperwork. There was a distinct possibility that I would see him.

I couldn't begin to imagine how that might go because he hadn't recognized me at the party.

Mason had not discerned that the girl he danced with on the balcony at the party—the girl in the red dress—was the same girl he'd met working on his airplane—the girl in the flight suit.

It was rather funny, really. Or at least it would be some day.

Right now I found it distracting. I caught myself watching for him. And maybe I spent a little more time on my hair and makeup in the mornings than I normally would.

I didn't know what I was going to do if he did cross my path out here. He was sure to recognize me.

Unless I happened to be wearing my flight suit... he probably wouldn't recognize me then. But he would surely recognize me in my business clothes and my hair down.

Then what would he think? He would have reason to feel deceived that the girl he thought was someone in his social circle, was actually a flight engineer. Supervisor, I reminded myself. I was a flight engineer supervisor.

If he was upset, he would have to deal with it. It wasn't my fault that he hadn't actually *seen* me beneath the airplane. He'd just seen a mechanical engineer at best or a maintenance technician at worst.

A Skye Travels Cessna came in for a landing and I watched as it taxied along the runway. It hadn't taken me long to become proficient at spotting the bright red Skye Travels logo splashed across the fuselage.

One day. One day I would see him again.

I could only imagine how that might go.

That didn't even begin to take into account the gypsy's fortune from all those years ago.

You will meet your soulmate underneath an airplane.

It was ridiculous. Absolutely ridiculous.

Over the years, I had imagined all sorts of ways that could happen. Meeting Mason beneath the plane had been so easy and simple. Not that he was the one the fortune teller spoke of even if I had believed her words. Which I most certainly did not.

I closed my computer and went down the hall for coffee. It wasn't that I liked the coffee down the hall, but I needed a break and coffee was a good enough excuse to leave my office.

Either that or I could wander down to the hangar. Check on the status of what the guys were working on. I liked to do that on occasion. They thought it was to keep them on their toes, but I just genuinely liked to see what they were doing.

They deserved no less after calling me out here away from the party.

In retrospect, I was probably better off not staying there. It would have been easy... far too easy... to get attached to Mason's undivided attention.

And that way lay madness.

Nothing good could come out of me even thinking about dating the grandson of Noah Worthington.

Ava had done her research and had figured out who, exactly, Mason was.

No, I decided as I poured coffee into a cup and added two packets of sugar. Nothing good could possibly come out of me thinking about Mason like this. People who worked at the same place I did, especially people who had some direct lineage to those who owned the company, were not a dating pool.

After I took a sip, I added another packet of sugar. It did nothing to keep the coffee from tasting like motor oil.

CHAPTER 18
Mason

PILOTS, by definition, knew lots of things about airplanes. And as so we could fix a whole lot of things that went wrong with them. Much like a man who drove a car. Some men could change tires, replace belts, and even figure out if a car needed a new alternator.

But there were things that men couldn't do when it came to fixing cars just as there were things pilots couldn't do when it came to fixing an airplane. And even if we did know what was wrong, we had to have parts and equipment to make those repairs.

That's why we had airplane engineers and mechanics.

And right about now, I was in need of someone whose sole job was to fix problems with airplanes.

The Cessna I'd flown to Whiskey Springs in had been fine. Until it wasn't.

I ran diagnostics. I did everything I knew to do.

But I was coming up empty-handed.

So I did what I had to do. I called Uncle Quinn and asked him to send an airplane engineer out here.

"Can't you fix it?" he asked.

"No," I said. "I've ruled out everything I know to rule out."

"Fine," Uncle Quinn said. "I'll send someone up there."

Uncle Quinn had a reputation of being a hard ass and he lived up to it, except not when his wife, Noelle, was around. When she was around, he became like putty in her hands. I'd really never seen anything like it.

"When?" I asked.

I could hear Uncle Quinn rolling his eyes. "I have to check the schedule. See who's available to fly up there. See which mechanic is available. It'll take me a few minutes. But today. Or tomorrow. Either today or tomorrow."

Good enough. It was more than I could hope for. I did not like feeling stranded. And with the airplane like it was, we weren't going anywhere at all. My passenger, Benjamin didn't seem to care one way or another. I didn't know what he was doing up here, but whatever it was, he seemed to have no stress.

I left my bed and breakfast and wandered downtown Whiskey Springs

It was a quaint little town in the heart of the Rocky Mountains.

Several of my cousins came here on a regular basis and I even had a cousin who lived here.

He wasn't home, of course, so I had lots of solitary wandering time. Or at least I would have if I hadn't wasted so much time trying to fix an airplane that needed someone who knew what they were doing.

I came across a little restaurant/bar called the Hungry Biscuit. A popular place, anytime I'd been there, it always had crowds. Right now, though, since it was barely ten o'clock in the morning, there was no line.

I ordered some coffee and found myself a seat by the window. I liked a good view whether it was a city skyline or snow-capped mountain peaks with low-hanging clouds.

Taking out my phone, I checked for messages.

Besides the usual text messages, I had four new alerts from the dating app I hadn't deleted yet.

It had occurred to me on the flight up to Whiskey Springs, that I just might find Chloé on the app.

Wouldn't that be convenient?

So I sipped coffee with cream and sugar and scrolled through the women who showed up in my app.

I looked at each one carefully. It helped that Chloé was blonde.

I saw a couple of women that I would consider dating if I hadn't already taken myself off the market.

There was a young lady named Ava, a pretty brunette, who looked like the kind of girl I might date if I actually dated. She reminded me a little bit of Chloé. I wasn't sure what it was. Her expression maybe.

At any rate, after I went through all the women on the app, I closed my eyes and held my finger over the delete button.

Then I changed my mind. The damn thing was too hard to set up. Besides it wasn't hurting anything.

I turned off the alerts to it and pushed my phone aside.

There. I could still look at it, but it would take more effort. The only reason I would be tempted to look at it anyway was to look for Chloé.

The more I thought about it, the odder the whole thing got to me. I avoided relationships with girls my family knew. Once they knew my family, knew who I was, it became difficult. Difficult for me to avoid them. I had made that mistake one time. I was a fast learner. That's why little black book was filled with girls who lived somewhere else.

But oddly enough, it wasn't like that with Chloé. Maybe it had been my mindset. When I'd gone to the party, I had been looking for a wife.

A message came in from Uncle Quinn.

UNCLE QUINN

Found a pilot and an engineer. Headed
your way.

Thank you.

Uncle Quinn grumbled a lot, but he took care of business.

Figuring I still had plenty of time, I ordered a burger and fries. No sense in missing lunch when there wasn't much else to do.

We'd get the airplane fixed and maybe, just maybe, with any luck at all, I could be out of here tomorrow. It all hinged on Benjamin and whatever he was doing. He did not seem like the kind of guy who lived by a schedule.

There wasn't much for a single guy to do in Whiskey Springs. I suppose I could go hiking, but even that wasn't fun to do alone.

So I ate my lunch in silence and thought about the two women I couldn't get out of my head.

One of them worked right there at Skye Travels. In the new hangar attached to the Skye Travels airport terminal. All I had to do was walk over to our hangar and find her. I did not even have to go outside. Grandpa made sure the two buildings were connected to keep people out of the weather, the heat more than anything else. Oddly enough, I didn't even know her name.

The other woman was a mystery. An enchanting young lady dressed in red. She had my heart the moment I saw her. I knew her name, but very little else about her.

They were so different. One would smell like jet fuel and knew how mechanical things worked—more so than I did. The other smelled like magnolias and had soft, delicate skin.

As I chewed a French fry, I wondered just why I would be thinking about two women who were so opposite of each other.

And there was something even more concerning.

They were starting to blur in my head.

61

CHAPTER 19

Chloé

As the plane left the ground, leaving nothing but a wobbly, floating sensation beneath us, I dug my fingers into the butter soft leather of the seat with one hand and held onto my four-point harness with the other.

Taking off was my least favorite part of flying. If I could fly without taking off, I would love flying.

It was probably the reason I never pursued a pilot's license. I'd certainly been in the air enough times. I'd even had guys give me the wheel.

But knowing how the electronic system worked was a completely different skill set from flying an airplane.

Since I preferred to avoid taking off as much as possible, it made sense that I focus on mechanical malfunctions and let others do the flying.

I relaxed my fingers some after we started to level off. It was a beautiful day for flying. The sky was blue with a few white wispy clouds. The sun was directly overhead, keeping everything bright, like an overhead light in a room. The roar of the engine should have been relaxing, but unfortunately, I was too well trained to listen for any little anomaly. It made flying a bit taxing.

One of the Skye Travels airplanes was having a technical problem that the pilot couldn't fix. So I was the one Quinn chose to send. I had the fleeting thought that Quinn might be testing me like the guys under my supervision did. But really, I was the logical person to send. I might be the latest hire, but I had the most training if not the most experience.

My pilot today was Jackson Fleming. Noah Worthington's son-in-law. I was flying with Jackson because today he just so happened to be flying to the little town outside of Denver where the airplane was. A place I'd never heard of. Whiskey Springs. Jackson had family there. Maybe a son. I wasn't sure.

At any rate, Jackson had a lot of flying hours under his belt and from I'd been told, he was one of the best.

I had ended up on Jackson's airplane with less than one hour's warning. I'd had just enough time to change into my flight suit and tuck my hair securely under my hat. I folded the clothes I'd worn to work and tucked them along with the extra set of clothes I kept in my overnight bag that I stored in my little closet in the office.

Since it was just after noon, Quinn couldn't guarantee that I would be back in Houston by the end of the work day. That didn't bother me so much. Working late was not unexpected. It was something I did when necessary.

I'm sure I'd feel differently one day when I had a husband and children waiting at home for me. But that particular someday seemed like a long time off. Maybe in another lifetime. A someday that would never get here.

Maybe I should take Ava's advice and put a profile on her favorite—and Mason's favorite—dating app. It wouldn't hurt to have a distraction from thinking about Mason. He wasn't someone I could realistically date for so many reasons, even if I wanted to. Which I did not.

Mason was a pilot and I didn't date pilots. I'd known too many of them over the few years I'd worked in aviation. I'd seen too many pilots—married and not—who took advantage of the freedom that came with a travel life style.

I hated to admit it but I'd been hit on more than a few times by those pilots. I never told anyone, not even Ava, but I had actually gone out with a guy only to find out that he had a wife and kids in another city. So one could say I had been burned.

It wasn't just pilots, though. I couldn't in all fairness put them in a playboy category all by themselves.

I sighed and watched the ground pass below. We were at ten thousand feet. Not too high to be able to see evidence of life below. I could see the blur of houses and roads. Rivers. The land reminded me of an impressionistic style painting. Much higher and everything got blurry. Like abstract art. Much lower than ten thousand feet and we were in what was considered the danger zone. There wasn't much room for error at the lower elevation.

At ten thousand feet the pilot had more flexibility of movement and could relax a bit. Knowing that bit of information helped me to relax a bit.

I'd left so quickly I hadn't even let Ava know where I was.

She and I usually texted at least once a day. We'd known each other for so long we were closer than sisters. I hardly ever talked to my older sister, sometimes once a week, sometimes only once a month. She had a husband and kids. A life so busy she was always seemed to be spinning in circles. Sometimes I envied her and sometimes, most times, I was thankful for my single lifestyle.

I settled back in my seat and closed my eyes. I could get used to flying in private jets, being the only passenger.

With the steady roar of the engine and Jackson Fleming at the controls, I dozed off a bit.

Even in my light sleep, I dreamed about a handsome pilot with a charming smile who, with just one glance, made my heart race.

And even in my sleep, I knew I was in trouble.
I could not stop thinking about Mason.

CHAPTER 20

Mason

I WAITED at the Whiskey Springs airport for my Uncle Jackson and the airplane engineer he was bringing with him.

Walking from my rental car to the brand-new terminal, I enjoyed the soft mountain air. Chipmunks darted up to me, stood on their hind legs to beg kindly, then raced off again when I had nothing for them.

The offending Cessna sat to one side, looking quite innocent. Like nothing at all was wrong with it. It was probably something simple going on with it, but damned if I could figure out what it was.

Today the rugged snow-capped peaks of the Rocky Mountains were hidden by white clouds that seemed to be attracted to them like cotton-candy to a wand.

After standing at the terminal for a few minutes, I checked the time on my watch then walked over to where I could look out over the valley.

A magnificent bald eagle glided easily on the air, swooping to the ground, looking for prey. I caught sight of a herd of bighorn from a movement to my right. They somehow walked along the steep mountainside without any problems. They had no fear. This was their land. They were just letting us use it for a time.

I rested my hip against a boulder and inhaled the light, clean air scented with spruce and fir trees. I could see why my grandfather had wanted to invest in building an airport terminal here.

It was lovely. And with the expanded runway, more planes could land here so more people could come here to enjoy this. Maybe I could buy a little cabin out here once I was married. We could fly up in the Phenom and spend the weekend. Maybe make some babies together.

I checked my watch again.

It was almost time for Uncle Jackson to be here.

I wanted the airplane fixed so I didn't have to entertain the idea of driving Benjamin to the Denver airport. If we couldn't get the plane fixed, we would have to either send another plane for him or pay for his commercial ticket. Paying for a commercial ticket was a last resort and I honestly couldn't remember us ever doing it. Skye Travels had a fleet of airplanes and pilots. There was always someone available, even if it was Grandpa himself.

I didn't mind staying in Whiskey Springs for a few days. Not really. I just would have preferred to have Chloé with me.

My old self always had a girl on standby. In fact, if I called Betty in Denver, she could and would be here for dinner.

That reminded me of something I could do. Something I'd been meaning to do.

I opened my phone and began to systematically delete names. I deleted Betty first. Then continued down my list.

I hadn't realized how many female contacts I had.

I was halfway through—I could have just deleted the folder, but I couldn't bring myself to do it—when I heard the airplane coming this way.

I hurried back to the terminal to wait. Uncle Jackson made a wide circle, then brought the plane in for a smooth as silk landing. He was one of the best.

He sat for a few minutes before taxiing toward the terminal.

I waited while he went through the post flight checklist.

As I waited, clouds drifted over the sunlight, taking away some of the brightness. I'd already learned that it rained every afternoon up here in the mountains.

Not much. Just a little shower. Just enough to get everything wet. Then it dried just as quickly.

Looked like that rain was about to fall. After a couple of drops landed on my arms, I stepped inside the building since there was no shelter.

A few minutes later, Uncle Jackson lowered the stairs of the plane and stepped down with a solid black umbrella over his head. The engineer, wearing a flight suit, followed, also carrying a black umbrella. Both of the umbrellas had the red Skye Travels logo on them. Most of the logos and advertising ideas came from my Aunt Brianna. She was the creative one in the family.

Uncle Jackson pressed a button, sending the stairs back up into the plane, spoke to the engineer, then hurried in my direction.

"Hey," he said.

"Hi. Thanks for doing this."

He shrugged. "I was headed this way anyway. Can you give me a quick ride into town?"

"What about the engineer."

"It's okay," he said. "the office is open. And we'll be right back."

"Sure."

We were halfway to town before it occurred to me that Uncle Jackson could have driven my car. It would have made a lot more sense because I hadn't even told the mechanical engineer what was wrong with the airplane.

He'd probably figure it out without my help. But still. It didn't seem right.

CHAPTER 21

Chloé

JACKSON TOLD me that he had to run into town, but someone
would be right back.

He offered to let me go with him, but I preferred to get
started on running my own diagnostics on the airplane.

By the time I'd made a quick look around the Cessna, the
rain had stopped. It seemed like a good time to start pulling my
equipment from Jackson's airplane. I didn't really know how
this remote repair thing was supposed to work. I had never done
a job like this before.

And that was on top of this being my first time in the Rocky
Mountains. The views were truly breathtaking.

It was amazingly quiet up here. No sounds other than the
breeze rustling through the aspen leaves and the scurry of little
chipmunks looking for food.

It was surreal to be working on an airplane without the
sounds of other airplanes coming and going in the background.

And although there was a faint scent of jet fuel in the air, I
could also smell pine and spruce trees. The air was so clean, it
was almost painful to breath. It smelled better than any candle in
any candle shop.

With the diagnostics running, I went inside the terminal.

There seemed to be only one person inside the building. A receptionist. According to her name plaque, her name was Jennifer. Jennifer looked to be in her fifties.

"Hello," Jennifer said when I walked inside. "You must be the airplane engineer."

"Yes," I said, returning her smile. "Can I just use your restroom?"

"Of course, Dearie," she said. "It's right across the hall and there's coffee if you want some."

I thanked her and after using the restroom, checked out the coffee machine. Unfortunately, it was like all the other coffee machines that airplane shops tended to have. Motor oil.

I poured some into a cup anyway and doctored it up with sugar and powered creamer.

It wasn't until after I took a sip and made a face that I realized Jennifer was watching me.

"It's terrible, isn't it?" she asked.

I wrinkled my nose. "I'm a latte girl."

"I understand completely. Let me get you something better."

"Oh no. Please don't go to any trouble."

But she had already picked up her phone and was texting someone.

"It's no trouble," she said with a smile.

"Thank you," I said. I wanted to pour out the coffee, but didn't know how to do it without being rude.

"Here," Jennifer said. "Let me take that and toss it for you."

"You're very kind," I said.

She waved away my compliment. "Us girls have to stick together," she said. "The men don't know about things like we do."

"I will agree that they don't seem to know much about coffee," I said.

Jennifer laughed. "Let me know if you need anything else, Hon. I won't leave you up here by yourself."

My eyes widened a bit. "Thank you." I hadn't thought about that. About being stranded up here in the middle of nowhere. From what I could tell, like most airports, this one was outside walking distance of town.

Since it wasn't anything I had to worry about at the moment, I put my head down and got to work.

CHAPTER 22
Mason

As I was dropping Uncle Jackson off in Whiskey Springs, I got a text message from Jennifer, the office manager at the airport.

JENNIFER

Would you bring a latte back for the engineer?

A latte?

A latte actually sounded pretty good right about now.

I stopped by the coffee shop and ordered two lattes.

With it being the beginning of the summer season, there were a lot of tourists in town. As a result, I had to wait in line for ten minutes. It seemed like a long time, but when I put it in perspective to waiting in long lines in Houston, it really wasn't so long.

While I was at it, I bought a half dozen scones. There was no telling how long we'd be at the airport and there was no delivery up there.

On impulse, I stopped by a fast food burger place before I left town and got two bags of French fries, too.

Surely that would hold a couple of guys over until we got back into town for dinner.

Even as the thought occurred to me, I realized that there was the faintest, remotest possibility that the engineer would be the girl.

But I quickly dismissed the thought. Knowing Uncle Quinn, he would send the supervisor, not just a technician. He wouldn't want to risk sending someone who didn't have much experience. He'd want the airplane fixed as quickly as possible.

It had been a pleasant thought and although it seemed like it would have put me in a good mood, it did the opposite.

I was honestly tired of being stuck here by myself. Grandpa insisted that I take a wife and although I had not liked the idea at first, it had grown on me and I was ready to make it happen. But I couldn't make it happen stuck out here in the middle of nowhere.

Whoever the engineer was, I'd help him get the plane repaired, then tomorrow I'd see if Benjamin was ready to head back to Houston. If he wasn't then I'd find a way to entertain myself here in Whiskey Springs. If he was going to be much longer, I would fly back to Houston, then come back when he was ready.

I did have one thing I could do while I was waiting around. I could call Aunt Noelle. Even if Uncle Quinn couldn't tell me who Chloé was, Aunt Noelle could find out. She would especially help me if I told her that I wanted to marry Chloé. On second thought, maybe I wouldn't tell her that. Everyone seemed to think it was a bad thing to disclose to people. I might be an idiot sometimes, but I was a fast learner.

I drove slowly across the gravel lot and parked near the terminal door. I got out of the car, leaned across the top, and looked toward the Cessna. I didn't see any sign of the engineer. No sign of any work going on.

Probably couldn't fix it. I ducked back inside the car,

grabbed the two lattes, the box of scones, and the bag of French fries and, after slamming the door with my foot, headed to the terminal door.

I was trying to hold everything—a bag, a box, and two coffees—and open the door without dropping anything.

I wasn't having much success and was just about to knock on the door with my elbow when it opened.

I stood face to face with... Chloé? The engineer?

It was Chloé with her long blonde hair framing her face. But she was wearing a flight suit. It was Chloé in a flight suit.

I saw recognition in her eyes followed quickly by acceptance.

But I just stood there, frozen, my brain struggling to sort out what I was seeing.

"Hi Mason," she said with a little smile, then took the coffees, box of scones, and the bag of fries from my arms.

I followed her inside the building.

After setting everything down, she turned and looked at me with a little smile. When I didn't say anything, she bit her lip.

"You're Chloé," I said.

She held out a hand. "I'm Chloé. Engineering supervisor."

"Chloé." I took her hand in mine. "Engineer."

Something flipped inside of me. Something so primal I couldn't even give it a name.

I'd been attracted to both Chloé in the red dress and the engineer. Chloé the engineering supervisor. One and the same.

And I, Mason Johnson, was at a loss for words.

CHAPTER 23

Chloé

MASON WAS one of the last people I expected to see at the Whiskey Springs airport.

All in all, I suppose it should not have been such a surprise since Mason's grandfather owned Skye Travels.

But still... out of all the possible ways and places I had imagined seeing him again, this had not been one of them.

I had taken my hat off after I came inside and let my hair fall loose around my shoulders. I had not, however, changed out of my flight suit. I'd decided that I would wait until I got back to Houston to change clothes.

"I brought you a latte," Mason said. "And some French fries."

Chloé smiled. "My favorites."

"You can use the break room," Jennifer said, looking from one of us to the other and back.

I gathered up the coffees and left the other things for Mason.

We sat across from each other at one of the tables in the break room.

"Are they the same?" I asked, looking at the coffee cups. They both had stickers covering the lid openings.

"Just alike," he said. "I got two of what I like."

I picked one and took a sip. "It's perfect."

He grinned like a little boy who had just successfully ridden a new bicycle by himself.

"I brought scones, too," he said. "And French fries."

"So you said."

I opened the bag with the French fries and laid them out on some paper napkins.

"I was starving," I said, biting into one. "These are good."

"They're from a little fast food place on the way here. Not a chain."

He opened the box of scones. "Try a scone," he said, holding the open box in my direction.

I took one. It was good, too.

"This is a good dinner," I said.

"We'll have dinner later," he said, off-handedly, like he'd just said something like Jennifer was still out front.

I stopped eating and just looked at him for a minute. He took a bite of scone.

"I think I'm supposed to fly back to Houston tonight."

Mason sat back. "Why would you do that? We have to fix the airplane."

I grinned. "No we don't."

"That's why you're here, right?" He looked over his shoulder, but there was no one else here. No one else who could fix the airplane.

"Of course," I said. "But It's done. It's fixed."

"How?"

"It was a computer thing," I said, waving it off. "Simple to fix..." Then I remembered that he had tried to fix it and that was why I was here. "With the right tools."

"So it's fixed." His expression was blank, leaving me unsure if he was happy or upset or neither.

"I can show you," I said.

He shook his head. "I don't need to see it. But you still can't fly back tonight."

"Why not?"

"I don't think Uncle Jackson is going back tonight and my passenger isn't ready to leave."

"The repairs sounded urgent," I said, trying to figure out what he was trying to say.

Was he saying that I was supposed to spend the night here tonight?

"Have you ever been stranded in the middle of nowhere?" he asked.

I considered that. "No. I don't think so." But it sounded like I was about to be.

"You'd know."

I bit back a laugh. The way he talked, we were somewhere in a cornfield. Not in the beautiful Rocky Mountains.

Then I shook my head.

"I can't stay," I said.

CHAPTER 24
Mason

I MUST HAVE a fairy godmother somewhere. And that fairy godmother had waved a magic wand in my direction.

I had not only found Chloé, I had found the engineer that I had met under the airplane.

And not only had I found them, they were one and the same.

The odds of all this coming together were too high for me to compute.

It wasn't chance. It was fate.

It had to be fate.

There were so many things we could do. We could go to dinner. We could walk around the little town and buy souvenirs. Maybe watch the sunset together.

But she wasn't cooperating.

"Really," she said. "I can't stay."

"But... why not?"

"I have to be there for my cat."

"Your what?"

"I can't leave my cat alone."

And everything crashed to the ground.

"You need to feed him?"

"Her. It's not that. She has food. I just can't leave her overnight."

"I thought cats were self-sustaining."

She looked at me sideways as she finished off the first bag of fries.

"You have obviously never owned a cat."

"My grandparents have cats."

"It's not the same thing," she said, shaking her head.

"If she's got food, what else could she need?"

"She's been sick and I have to give her medication."

I didn't know what to say. I had found the girl of my dreams and we were in a lovely place. And yet she couldn't stay.

"Can someone else do it?" I asked.

She seemed to consider this. "My friend Ava. Maybe."

"Can you ask her?"

She seemed to consider. "What if she can't? Then I have to get home."

"Ok," I said. "Just ask. If she says no, then I'll fly you home. Tonight."

"What about your passenger?"

"He'll have to wait until I get back tomorrow."

She sipped her coffee. "And Jackson isn't leaving tonight? Quinn actually said that I could be home tonight even if it wasn't by the end of day."

I leaned back in my chair and made a decision. This was the girl I was going to marry. It was my job to make her happy.

"Don't worry," I said. "I'll get you home. We'll take the Cessna since it's fixed. Then I'll bring it back in the morning. If my passenger wants to leave tomorrow, it'll just be a quick turn around."

"That's a lot of flying," she said, her brow creased with worry.

I shrugged. "I'm a pilot. It's what I do."

"I guess so," she said.

We finished eating in silence.

"Want to at least see Whiskey Springs before you leave?" I asked.

"Yes," she said before I barely got the question out.

I grinned. "Let's go then. We can have dinner at this restaurant I found."

"Didn't we just eat?" she asked, tossing the wrappers in the trash.

"An appetizer," I said. "Besides we have to eat at a place called the Hungry Biscuit."

She laughed out loud. Then seemed to catch herself. "I'm sorry. That's just a funny name."

"But they have really good food."

"Okay," she said. "Why not?"

I was liking this girl more and more. *Why not?* was my favorite answer to so many things.

CHAPTER 25
Chloé

MASON OPENED the car door and closed it behind me. Then he got into the driver's side and slid his shades over his eyes.

My job here was finished. It really had been simple, but I didn't want to stress that too much. I didn't want him to feel bad that he hadn't been able to do the repairs.

It was only late afternoon, but the sunlight was fading quickly. It must be a mountain thing since I hadn't seen any rain in the forecast.

The drive into Whiskey Springs took us twenty-five minutes, but mostly because the roads were narrow and windy. Mason had to slow down on the curves. Even with the guardrails, it was a bit unsettling.

"I've learned a lot about the town since I got here two days ago," he said. "They go all out for Christmas. It's like a real-live Hallmark movie around here."

"I wouldn't mind seeing that," I said.

"We'll come here then," he said. "Spend a few days during the holidays."

I looked at him sideways. Maybe there was something wrong with him.

"Christmas is a long way off," I said.

"Nah. It'll be here before we know it."

"Do you always do that?"

"Do what?" he asked.

"Nothing," I said. I would have found it endearing if I had known him for more than a minute. As it was, he was making me a little nervous. Making me wonder if he was this way with all the girls.

His reassurances that we would do things together actually made me think the opposite. It made me think that he said things out of reflex.

I sent Ava a quick text while he drove.

She didn't answer right away. That usually meant she was on a date.

If Ava was on a date, I shouldn't ask her to take care of my cat.

But the way things were looking, I really might not make it home tonight. I shouldn't have come into town with him. I should have insisted that he fly me home.

The thing was, I wasn't ready to leave yet. As much as I knew in my head that he was bad for me, I was drawn to him like a moth to a flame.

"Did you hear from your friend?" Mason asked.

"She's on a date." I wasn't for sure that Ava was on a date, but decided that it got Ava off the hook. Just in case.

"Oh," he said. Then. "It's okay. It's not that far up here."

Even though I worked around pilots and airplanes every day, I had not adopted their perspective on distances. It seemed to me like Whiskey Springs, Colorado was a rather long way from Houston.

He parked in a pay parking lot off of Main Street.

"I'll come around," he said before hopping out of the car. He was already opening my door before I realized what he was talking about.

Chivalry, it seemed, was not dead. Instead, it lived in the form of what my gut told me was a playboy pilot.

And even though I prided myself on maintaining my distance from his kind, it seemed I was just as susceptible as the next girl.

I was crushing hard on Mason Johnson.

CHAPTER 26

Mason

IT WAS the beginning of the tourist season in Whiskey Springs and the streets were crowded to prove it.

I could have parked in the Hungry Biscuit parking lot, but I wanted as much time with Chloé as possible. Parking on the other end of town required us to walk along Main Street melding in with the other tourists to get there.

Tourists stood in the street snapping pictures with their phones of the sunset setting over the mountains. Bright red and orange colors splashed across the sky and spilled onto the rugged mountains peaks, softening them with a muted glow.

Rowdy music spilled from the door of a saloon as we passed. The Whiskey Springs Saloon.

"A saloon?" Chloé asked as we passed.

"It's also a hotel and a restaurant. Want to see?"

"I am a bit curious," she said, peaking past me to see inside the door.

"Come on," I said, taking her hand and leading her in through the door. This was something everyone should experience.

A saloon girl dressed in a ruffled bright blue and white dress in the nineteenth century western style sat at a piano at the far corner, playing with lively animation. Other girls dressed similarly scurried her and there, waiting on tables.

Regular customers like us, wearing jeans and t-shirts and other modern clothes, sat at those tables around the room.

Pulling Chloé along behind me, I walked right past the tables up to the bar. The bar was a monstrous mahogany with a smooth as glass top. There were a couple of guys sitting on stools with beer bottles in front of them.

"Howdy Mason," the barkeeper said.

"Hello Peter. Can we get a couple of whiskeys?"

After Peter nodded and walked off, Chloé turned to me. "You know the barkeeper?"

I shrugged. "I have a room here."

"Oh," she said. She had no idea how easy she was to ruffle or how cute she was when I managed to throw her off guard.

"They have hotel rooms upstairs," I explained.

"Nice," she said, looking up toward the balcony. I could see the suspicion all over her face.

"They are," I said. "Really nice. Nineteenth century historical with updated conveniences."

"Hmm." She did not look convinced.

Peter brought two glasses of whiskey and slid them over in front of us.

Chloé sniffed hers and wrinkled her nose. Then she looked at me. "Whiskey?"

I leaned over to whisper. "You don't have drink it. It's a prop. You know. For the experience."

"You're weird," she said.

I laughed. "So I've been told. But think about it. Whiskey Springs. Whiskey."

"Right." She brought the glass to her lips and took a tiny taste. I knew she drank champagne, so whiskey wouldn't be THAT much different.

She glanced at my untouched glass.

"Are you going to drink yours?"

"Not if I'm flying you back tonight," I said. "At least twelve hours bottle to throttle."

She nodded. I wasn't sure if she knew what that meant, but being around pilots, she should have some idea.

"A prop. For the experience." She tasted it again, then looked at me with those beautiful green eyes I hadn't been able to stop thinking about. In retrospect I should have seen that they were one and the same. The same green enchanting eyes in both Chloé in the red dress and Chloé the engineer. No wonder I had been troubled and confused.

Holding her whiskey in one hand, she twirled around on the stool with her back to the bar and studied the restaurant.

"We should definitely eat here one night," she said.

I followed suit and turned around, too, grinning from ear to ear.

My girl was coming around to the spirit of things.

CHAPTER 27

Chloé

I WAS REMINDED of the old saying. *If you can't beat them, join them.*

I'd never had much need to use the old adage until now.

Having never been in a place even remotely similar to this, I was captivated. All they needed was a gunfight on the street and it would feel like we were right there on the set of a western movie.

The rowdy music. The conversation. The clink of glass against glass behind the bar. All swirled together to create a place spilling over with authenticity. Especially if I closed my eyes and ignored the car motors outside.

As for Mason, I'd decided the best way to figure out what he was up to was to join his game.

When I suggested that we eat here *one night*, implying not tonight, but a night in the future, he just grinned.

The only thing that had really flustered him was finding me standing at the airport terminal door.

It had been more than a little unsettling, even for me, and I knew who he was. I couldn't imagine how surprised he must have been to find me there. The me who had worn the red dress to the party then vanished Cinderella style.

As I watched, not drinking the whiskey, just holding it for a prop, like Mason suggested, a well-dressed couple came downstairs. The man was dressed in a suit and the woman was wearing a knee-length sparkly cocktail dress.

I closed my eyes and groaned.

"What's wrong?" Mason asked, taking the whiskey from my hand and setting it aside. "Are you ill?"

I shook my head, then took a deep breath, and opened my eyes.

"I should have changed clothes," I said, my voice barely a whisper. "I look like a dork."

"You look adorable," he said.

I rolled my eyes at him.

"Other women only wish they could pull that off," he said.

"That's not helping."

"What will?" he asked.

"I don't know." The couple walked past us on the way to their table and the woman flicked her eyes down to my boots as she neared. Then she looked over at Mason.

I wanted to crawl beneath the bar. Her expression all but said *What's a guy like that doing with a girl like you?*

Somewhere in the back of the haze of humiliation, I heard Mason set his glass down.

Then he leaned over, put his fingers lightly on my chin, and kissed me full on the lips. The kiss was light, but still, it was a kiss.

My humiliation changed to shock.

Mason was sending my emotions all over the place.

Pulling back, he smiled into my eyes. "Let her chew on that," he whispered.

I blinked, then glanced over my shoulder at the woman who had given me that scathing glance.

"I don't think she saw," I said.

"She saw," Mason said. "And you can bet she wishes she could look as sexy as you in a flight suit."

He was daft.

But he made me smile.

"Ready to blow this popsicle stand?" he asked.

"I'm with you," I said. And no statement had ever been more true.

Mason had me in the palm of his hand. My only hope was that he didn't know it.

CHAPTER 28

Mason

"I HAVE AN IDEA," I said as we walked down the crowded Main Street, hand in hand.

I was a simple man with simple reasoning. Now that I had kissed her, it seemed only natural that I would back up and hold her hand.

"What's that?" she asked as we sidestepped a group of teenage girls carrying ice cream cones. "You want ice cream?"

"Maybe later," I said, laughing. "Come on."

I led her into a little store. I'd gone in here yesterday to look around, but hadn't bought anything. Still. I knew where things were.

I went straight to the back and, releasing her hand, pulled out a cute pink leather jacket. Zippers. Only a little fringe. There were limits.

It might not be something anyone would wear in Houston, but here in Whiskey Springs, it was adorable.

"Try this on."

After helping her into the buttery soft leather jacket in soft pale pink that fell to her hips, I pulled her equally soft blonde hair from the collar and let it cascade down her back.

"Perfect." Taking her shoulders, I turned her toward the nearest mirror. The jacket turned her flight suit into a cute, fashionable outfit. "Do you like it?"

"I love it," she said, reaching for the price tag.

"Nuh-uh." I said, taking her hand. "It's a gift."

"You can't—"

"Don't be silly," I said. "Do you want anything else?"

I started toward the checkout counter.

"Maybe later," she said, then pulled on my hand to stop me. "At least get you something, too."

I grinned. "Okay. What should I get?"

I felt more than saw the devious expression flash across her features.

She pulled me to the other side of the store. Then stood with her hands on her hips.

Reaching over, she pulled a white cowboy hat off the shelf.

I groaned to myself as she set it on my head.

"Good guys always wear white," she said with devilment in her tone.

Grinning, I settled the cowboy hat on my head. "So I'm a good guy, am I?"

It didn't matter that I had never worn a cowboy hat before. It was worth it to hear her call me one of the good guys.

It made no sense, really. Such a small thing. But looking into her smiling face, I wanted her to see nothing other than good in me and if wearing a white cowboy hat was what it took, a white cowboy hat I would wear.

"This one?" I asked, turning my head this way and that.

"Perfect."

"Wait here," I said, in what I hoped was a surreptitious move, snapped the price tag from her jacket and approached the counter.

"I'd like to buy this for the lady," I said, sliding the price tag across the counter. "And this for me." I removed my hat and placed it, too, on the counter.

She looked over her wire-rimmed glasses at Chloé. She acted like she had never discreetly checked anyone out before. But I just aimed my most charming grin at her and she went about ringing me up. I scanned my credit card and we were on our way.

Chloé, in her new pink leather jacket and me in my white cowboy hat. Walking hand in hand.

CHAPTER 29

Chloé

I DECIDED Mason was a bit eccentric. And at the same time extremely thoughtful.

Now that I had a leather jacket over my flight suit, I didn't stick out like a sore thumb.

As Mason and I walked along Main Street, dodging tourists —I couldn't bring myself to think of us as tourists—it was hard to not think about how he had kissed me.

Kissed me. Right there in front of everyone.

Cognitively I knew why he kissed me right then and there. It was his way of telling the woman looking down her nose at me that I was not to be looked at like that. That I was kissable.

Emotionally, I was undone.

There were so many things I wanted to ask Mason.

We passed an art shop that I wouldn't mind visiting one day. The west, I was discovering, was a lot like a foreign country. The art was different. The style of dress was different. The words were different. I'd heard more than one person say pop when referring to soda. And I'd only been here for a handful of hours.

I hadn't recognized any of the brands in the store either. But Mason seemed at home no matter where I happened to see him.

Here. At a fancy party in Houston. In an airplane hangar beneath an airplane.

As we reached the Hungry Biscuit, the sun had dropped below the mountains, casting everything into a sudden darkness. Nothing like the Houston sunset that lasted forever or the Pittsburg sunset that seemed to linger over the three rivers even after it dropped over the horizon.

Since there was already a line, he took a pager and we found an empty bench outside. We sat side by side tucked beneath a blue spruce tree. Now that the sun was down, I was doubly thankful for my jacket.

"This would make a nice Christmas tree," I said.

"They probably decorate it," he said.

"Do you come here a lot?" I asked. It wasn't really one of the things I wanted to know, but it seemed like a good place to start.

"It's my first time."

"You're kidding."

Shaking his head, he looked away. "No. Usually when I visit someplace new, I use the time to explore. To get a feel for the place. I haven't done as much here because I spent a lot of time working... unsuccessfully... on the Cessna."

"You seem like you know a lot about Whiskey Springs."

"I guess it's my hidden talent," he said, turning back and smiling at me. He put an arm around my shoulders and pulled me against him.

Now I couldn't ask him the things I wanted to know. it would just be too awkward.

"What about you?" he asked. "What's your hidden talent?"

"I don't think I have one."

"Everybody has one," he said. Then he abruptly changed the subject. "Did you hear from Ava?"

"I don't know." I pulled my phone out of my handbag. "Yes."

AVA

What's up? You okay?

I quickly sent an answer.

You won't believe it. I'm in Colorado.

AVA

Hot date?

I glanced over at Mason. Yes.

No. Work. Hey. Can you possibly give Kit Kat her antibiotic tonight? In case I have to stay over.

Thought bubbles.

AVA

Sure. Consider it done.

Awesome. Send me a picture please!

She would do it. I trusted Ava more than anyone else. Even with Kit Kat. And that was saying a lot.

Mason was scrolling on his own phone, his way of giving me privacy, I suppose. I had to make a decision. If I told him the truth, then I would be spending the night here. If I didn't, then as soon as we left here, we'd be driving back to the airport and flying to Houston.

He saw me looking at him and grinned.

"She said she would do it," I blurted.

I really had no choice.

I had fallen under Mason's spell.

All the more reason to find out why his dating app bio declared an intent to find a wife.

Even Ava, who regularly used the app, found it highly irregular.

"Super," Mason said, giving me a quick squeeze.

"I don't have a place to stay."

"Don't worry. I'll take care of that."

I didn't know how exactly he was going to take care of it. "Don't I need to—"

My phone chimed with another message, interrupting what I was going to ask him.

> AVA
> Did you ask him yet?

> What are you talking about?

> Mason. Did you ask him yet?

There was no way Ava knew I was with Mason. She knew me, but she was not psychic. She was guessing.

"Did you ask me what?" Mason asked, looking over at my phone.

CHAPTER 30
Mason

"Nothing," Chloé said quickly, the blood rushing to her cheeks in a fetching blush.

I left it alone. I should not have been eavesdropping on her text conversation. I'd find out later what she and her friend were talking about.

I actually had lots of things to take care of anyway, now that I had managed to get her to stay.

"I'll text Uncle Quinn and let him know that you won't be in tomorrow."

She put a hand over mine.

"I think I should do that."

"Right," I said. Right. It was her job. And not my place to take control.

Our pager went off. "Our table is ready," I said, standing up and holding out a hand for her.

Chloé looked absolutely charming in her pink leather jacket. No one would be looking at my girl all funny any more. I'd make sure of that.

The hostess led us to a table in the back—at my request sweetened with a little tip.

I held her chair as she sat, then sat next to her.

Her hands clasped in front of her, resting on the table, she looked at me.

"Would you like a martini?" I asked.

"Yes," she said, clearly surprised. "extra olives."

I ordered two martinis.

"How did you know I like martinis?"

"Just a guess," I said. "Another one of my super powers."

"You're starting to scare me a little bit."

I laughed. "I'm harmless."

She nodded slowly.

"Maybe."

"What's bothering you?" I asked. "Except that I made a lucky guess."

"Nothing," she said.

The server brought our drinks, then left us alone.

Chloé went straight for the toothpick with olives.

"I need to text Quinn," she said.

"And I need to call the saloon. Hotel." I amended at her look.

I called the saloon. Added another room to my reservation. It was the last room Peter had.

After Chloé texted Uncle Quinn, she put her phone aside.

"All our work is done," I said.

She leaned back, taking a deep breath. "I guess it is."

"What is it you were going to ask me?"

"Was I going to ask you something?"

"I think you were." I put a hand on hers, lightly rubbing my thumb against her soft skin. Chloé the engineer's hands were identical to those of Chloé the socialite.

I smiled to myself. Of course they were. She was one and the same.

"What's funny?" she asked.

"Nothing," I said. "I'm here in a beautiful place with a beautiful woman. Life could not be better."

The server came by. Brought us some chips and dip. The song changed to something soft. Romantic.

"My friend, Ava," she said. "Found your profile on a dating app."

CHAPTER 31

Chloé

I HAD NOT PLANNED to tell him. Truly I wasn't going to.

I didn't want him to think that I was looking to get married.

But, I reminded myself, I hadn't found him on a dating app. I had simply kept running into him. Then he was the one who had convinced me to stay in Whiskey Springs overnight.

I had no reason to think that he would think that I was pursuing him.

Because I was not.

I was most certainly not pursuing him.

Even if he had kissed me.

Even if I wanted him to kiss me again.

Still. He looked at little bit... regretful.

"It's a long story," he said.

"You don't have to tell me," I said. "In fact, I really don't want to know."

He tilted his head and appeared to study me.

"It was before I met you," he said. "Sort of."

I didn't want him to tell me, really, but now I was curious. And it looked he was going to tell me anyway.

"What do you mean sort of?"

"It was after I talked to you when you were working on my Phenom, but before I met you at the party."

"Wait." I held up a finger. "Your Phenom?"

He grinned. "One day," he said. "It will be one day."

I narrowed my eyes at him. "I'm thinking maybe you should tell me this story after all."

"I agree as it's rather convoluted."

I sighed. Everything about him was convoluted.

"It all started on my birthday. Last Thursday." He twirled his martini glass, watching the swirling liquid, while he spoke.

"The day we met... underneath the airplane." *Just like the fortune teller said.*

He nodded.

He only thought it started that day. What he didn't know was it actually started long before that. It actually started when I was fourteen years old and Ava dragged me into a fortune teller's tent.

I'd been haunted by that encounter ever since.

You'll meet your soulmate underneath an airplane.

She could have said *on an airplane.* That would have been so much more normal.

But... no.

It had to be something so bizarre that it couldn't possibly happen, even by chance.

Until it did.

But he was telling me more. Possibly everything.

"My grandfather gives us all something special on our thirtieth birthdays. And my special thing is a Phenom, but I can't have it yet."

"So he bought you a gift, but he won't give it to you."

"Not yet. He wants me to get married first."

I put my hands on the table to steady myself. I was feeling slightly faint.

"So it's true," I said, not quite meeting his gaze.

I looked away, having suddenly lost my appetite. I had hoped that it had not been true. That he had put it on the app by mistake or maybe even as a joke. A joke would be good since women were always the ones looking for husbands on those things.

Not men.

Men didn't look for wives.

It went against their nature.

CHAPTER 32

Mason

CHLOÉ EXCUSED herself for the restroom.

I got the sense that I had said something to upset her.

I was merely trying to tell her the story of how I came to need a wife.

It was very unusual in the modern world for a man to need a wife. Something people did in the old days.

Uncle Dylan had warned me against telling anyone.

But I'd already gone and told the world through that dating app. I should have deleted it. I knew I should have deleted it.

The server brought us fresh chips even though we had barely touched the old ones.

While I waited I decided to check in with Uncle Quinn.

> Chloé got the airplane fixed.

> UNCLE QUINN
> So she said. I knew she would.

I stared at my phone. Uncle Quinn had known all alone who she was. He'd known when he introduced us that she worked for Skye Travels.

It didn't bother me that she worked there. I worked for Skye Travels, too.

> I got her a room at the saloon for the night.

Thought bubbles.
Then they stopped.

> Something else?

UNCLE QUINN

> Never mind. Just don't do anything stupid.

Right. Why did Uncle Quinn think I would do something stupid?

Probably because he didn't know I was a changed man. He couldn't possibly know that I had changed my playboy ways and was practically a married man.

I slid an olive off the toothpick in my drink and decided that he couldn't possibly know this.

He would know about the requirement for me to find a wife, but he wouldn't know that I was taking it seriously.

Didn't matter. They would all find out soon enough. Grandpa Noah couldn't ask something like that of me—of anybody—and not expect it to be done.

In fact... I went ahead and deleted the dating app. It only took a second.

Seconds later, Chloé came back to the table.

"You okay?" I asked.

"I'm not sure," she said.

"You need to eat."

"Maybe."

I signaled for the server to come and take our orders.

"What would you like?" I asked her.

"I'll have whatever you're having." She tried to smile, but it faltered.

I ordered burgers and fries for us then after the server left, I leaned forward.

"Chloé," I said. "I deleted the dating app."

"Why would you do that?" she asked. "I thought you needed to find a wife."

"I do need to find a wife, but the app had been a bad idea."

She shrugged, but there was something in her eyes that looked a lot like hurt.

"Do you have a girlfriend?" she asked. "Someone you've been dating that you can marry."

"No," I said. "I don't have anyone I can marry."

"What are you going to do then?"

"I was thinking I'd marry you."

CHAPTER 33
Chloé

I HAD HEARD HIM WRONG.

I thought Mason said he was going to marry me.

"I'm sorry," I said. "It's noisy in here. I'm having some trouble hearing."

"I said I was thinking I'd marry you." There was a loud sound that sounded a lot like someone dropped a tray of dishes, coming from the kitchen that muffled his voice.

"What?"

"Marry me."

Just as he said the words, a hush had settled over the restaurant—a reaction to the noise from the kitchen.

So the noise level went from very loud to very quiet in an instant.

And Mason just so happened to say those two words when it went quiet.

Now all the guests at the other tables were looking at us. Watching us expectantly. Waiting for my answer.

"Get on one knee," someone shouted.

"Ask her the right way," someone else said.

Mason looked at them.

"Come on, Man," someone said. "Do the thing."

Do the thing?

I shook my head.

"It's okay," I said, stretching out a hand toward him. "They heard you wrong."

He shook his head. "They didn't."

People were still watching us. I was so glad I was wearing the leather jacket and wasn't just wearing my flight suit. Mason had on a pants and a dress jacket. We would have looked like we didn't belong together. Did we look like we belonged together now? People in the restaurant seemed to think so.

I looked back at Mason.

He slid out of his chair and went down on one knee in front of me.

"No," I said. "You don't have to do this."

"Chloé," he said. "I know I haven't known you long, but I've known since I met you at the party. Maybe I knew before that and just wasn't thinking. But you're the one I want to marry."

"No," I said, putting a hand on his shoulder. I leaned forward, keeping my voice low. "You don't have to do this."

I was telling Mason Johnson not to propose to me. I was out of my mind.

Even as I was asking him not to do it, my heart was soaring like the eagle I had seen earlier.

And at the same time, my head was reeling with disbelief. This had to be a mistake.

"It's not a mistake," he said. "I want you to be my wife."

A chorus of voices came from the other customers. Everyone was watching us.

"Say yes!"

"Kiss her!"

"Where's the ring?"

"I don't have a ring yet," he said. "but I'll get you one. Whatever you like."

"Say yes!"

Ignoring the people watching us, I kept my hands on Mason's shoulders and searched his sparkling blue eyes.

For whatever reason, he had decided that I was the girl he wanted to marry.

It made no sense to me. But I didn't not want to marry him.

I just didn't understand.

And it would be just downright insensitive to tell him no in front of all these people.

I had no choice. I could either agree to marry the man I was crushing on or I could crush his heart or at the very least embarrass him.

"Yes," I said, loud enough for everyone to hear me. "Yes. I'll marry you."

People clapped. A man actually cheered.

Grinning from ear to ear, Mason pulled me into his lap and hugged me close.

Our audience went back to doing whatever they had been doing before. Our moment in the spotlight was over.

Didn't matter. Because then he kissed me and I forgot that anyone else was in the world.

CHAPTER 34
Mason

I WAS a firm believer in fate.

Fate had introduced me to Chloé and then had put us in the same place at the same time. On more than one occasion.

That was not to be ignored.

Everything seemed to have aligned so perfectly.

I hadn't had any doubt from the very beginning that she was the one and I didn't have any doubt now.

She did. But that was understandable. I had not had time to court her properly.

I'd planned on easing her into the idea, but sometimes it was better to just jump right in with both feet. Everything else would take care of itself.

She didn't eat much. I could see the wheels turning in her head. I, on the other hand, ate my food and some of hers.

I was happy. I had done it. And it had been so much easier than I had expected.

I was engaged.

And not to just anybody. I was engaged to someone I actually liked spending time with. I had been afraid that I was going to have to marry someone I could simply tolerate. I should have known better. That's not what Worthingtons did. Worthingtons married their soulmates.

Chloé and I had so much in common.

I flew airplanes. She worked on airplanes.

We both like studying the weather.

We both like lattes and French fries.

We both liked martinis.

It sounded like about as good a foundation as a lot of people had. And I'm sure there were other things, too.

Things we didn't even know to think about yet.

I liked just looking at her.

And I liked kissing her.

Kissing her was the best part.

We lingered a little bit at the table, but I was ready to get back to the saloon. To make sure Peter had our rooms reserved the way I'd asked.

We walked hand-in-hand in the soft evening moonlight along the now not so crowded Main Street.

There were still a few people out, mostly couples, like us, taking a moonlight stroll.

The comparison gave me happiness. I'd taken a lot of moonlight strolls with a lot of different women. But Chloé was different.

With Chloé I could see a future. I could imagine us walking along this same street a few years from now, a couple of toddlers, one in my arms, the other walking already, holding Chloé's hand, maybe even one in stroller. In my imaginary world, we were quite busy.

"What are you thinking about?" she asked as we passed the store where we had bought her leather jacket.

"Not so much," I said, pulling our clasped hands to my lips and lightly kissing her fingers. "Just thinking about how grateful I am for my grandfather. I'm grateful that he nudged me out of my ways."

"Look," she said, stopping right there on the street and looking into my eyes. "You don't have to do this."

She stopped long enough to take a deep breath. "I can help you find someone to marry."

"You don't like me," I said, my heart crashing into a thousand shards. I knew what she was doing. I'd done it many times myself.

She shook her head. "It's not that. I like you a lot. But... I'm not right for you."

"I've used that one before," I said, mostly to myself.

"No," she said. "I *work* on airplanes. I don't fly in them and I don't even pilot them."

"Oh," I said. "Is that all?"

I swept a lock of hair out of her face, then took both her hands and looked deep into her eyes.

"You don't understand," I said. "I don't care about that. I've dated socialites." I took a breath. "I'll teach you how to fly."

She smiled. "Okay."

We continued down the street, but there was a sadness in her eyes.

I didn't understand it.

I might not ever understand it, but I made it my mission right then and there to do whatever I could to take that sadness out of her eyes.

CHAPTER 35

Chloé

I STOOD in my hotel room, looking out over the window at the deserted street below. It was almost eleven o'clock, so there weren't very many people out and about.

Someone had brought my travel bag to the hotel. I don't know who it was, but I had found it sitting right there on the bed after I used the large silver key to unlock the door to my room.

Having my luggage delivered without even having to ask for it, much less having to go get it myself, was part of that world Mason lived in. He thought nothing of such things. They were simply part of life as he knew it.

Take the fresh flowers on the dresser. There was a note. *Chloé, We hope you enjoy your stay. Please call the number on this card if you need anything at all.* I would bet money that most people didn't get fresh flowers with personalized notes in their rooms.

But being a guest of Noah Worthington's grandson put me in the group who had their luggage brought from their private jet and fresh flowers brought to their room.

No one knew that I was simply here to repair the airplane.

Sure, I'd flown to Whiskey Springs on a private jet, but only because I was here to do a job.

Then somehow in the course of a few hours, I had become Mason's fiancé.

There was a simple explanation. He was confused.

He thought he wanted to marry me, but after he had time to think about it, he would come to his senses and realize that I wasn't right for him.

My phone chimed. It didn't chirp. It chimed.

I had a text message from my old boss in Pittsburgh. His name was David Smith. David had taught me everything I knew that didn't come from textbooks. In fact, he had taken what the textbooks had taught me and brought it to life. The textbooks had merely provided a foundation. There was so very much more to learn.

David called it experience and he had given it to me. I would always be beholden to him.

DAVID
Hey Chloé. I hope you're well. We miss you.

Miss you guys, too.

I dropped the phone to the bed and plopped down next to it.

While Ava was getting dates, I got messages from work.

Something didn't seem right about that.

Staring at the door the separated our rooms, I realized I found it comforting that Mason was right next door. He'd kissed me lightly before ushering me into my room.

"I'll be right next door if you need me," he said.

I'd smiled and closed the door.

Everything about being engaged to Mason was convoluted.

Yet I needed to talk to somebody. I sent Ava a message.

114

> Did you give Kit Kat her medicine?

She wrote back immediately.

AVA

> Yes, but I don't think she likes me anymore.

I put a hand over my mouth and laughed at the picture she sent me. Kit Kat was sitting in the kitchen floor looking up at Ava with obvious distrust.

> As long as she got it down.

AVA

> It's down. We both managed to survive.
> Heading home. Talk later.

Then a another message came in from David.

DAVID

> Haven't been able to fill your job. If you ever want to come back, your job is still here.

> You shouldn't tell me that.

I could practically see him shrugging.

DAVID

> But it's true. Can't change the truth.

I smiled. I missed David and his crew. I missed Pittsburgh. Even though I missed it, I was really trying to make a home in Houston.

> They offered me the job here. Full time.

> Of course they did. They know you're the best.

How would they know that?

I gave you a glowing reference. Told them I
didn't want you to leave here.

Wow. Now I felt terrible for leaving my old job. But David understood. He knew that I wanted a supervisor position. And he wasn't going to be giving up his position for years to come. He knew, and even encouraged me to go someplace where I could get promoted quickly. When the temporary position in Houston opened up, he had been the one to find out about it and he encouraged me to take it.

"You never know," he'd said. "it could turn into something really good for you."

I doubted he expected it to turn into something permanent quite so quickly. I know I hadn't.

Although I had quickly accepted the job at Skye Travels, I still had emotional ties to my job in Pittsburgh.

I could go back there. It wasn't too late.

I looked toward the door that separated our rooms. Blue. The door was blue.

Mason was asking me to leave the life I knew. Not by just leaving my job, but by leaving my life as I knew it. He was asking me to learn to fly airplanes and not just work on them. He would want children.

I wanted children. Having children fell into that someday world that never came.

I needed to take a walk. I did my best thinking when I was moving. After putting my jacket back on, I grabbed my phone and room key and headed downstairs.

There were only a few people left in the restaurant, mostly sitting at the bar, but the girl, a different one now, played the piano, keeping the music going.

I stepped outside into the startling cold wind and walked left toward the residential area.

I turned left on Alexander street and walked down the sidewalk beneath the blue spruce and fir trees. It was like walking through a Christmas tree lot, only the scent was stronger. The trees smelled stronger in their natural habitat and, of course, with their roots still attached.

The houses on this particular street that I wandered were not small houses. They were actually large houses, some with lights still on. I imagined the families inside. The children sleeping. The adults sitting in front of the fireplace. Maybe reading or having a glass of wine.

Some of the houses had probably been here for hundreds of years. They would have seen so many changes. So many people had come and gone.

But the houses were still here.

I'm not sure what it was and I might not ever know, but something resonated in me as I walked along the tree-lined residential streets of Whiskey Springs.

Maybe it was a magic in the air. Something too faint to be detected by mere humans.

But I knew what I needed to do.

CHAPTER 36
Mason

I WAS RATHER pleased with myself, all things considered. I had escorted Chloé to her room in a most admirable gentlemanly fashion.

And I had gone to my own room for the evening. There was a time... a couple of weeks ago perhaps... that I would have dropped her off at her room, then gone back downstairs to roam around for other female company.

But I did not do that.

I downloaded that book Grandpa had recommended onto my iPad and settled into bed to read.

After reading a couple of pages, I could already see that it was going to be a good book.

I sent Grandpa a quick text and thanked him for recommending it. Told him that I was enjoying reading it.

I rested my iPad on my chest and, clasping my hands behind my head, studied the door between that separate my room from Chloé's.

I wanted to be married quickly. Not because of the Phenom, at least not totally, but because, well, I just wanted to be married to Chloé.

Somewhere along the way, getting married had shifted and was no longer about the airplane at all, I mused.

The thought of marrying anyone else was unthinkable and I wondered if I would be more opposed to Grandpa Noah's terms if I weren't so smitten with Chloé.

I think that the Phenom was actually giving me the excuse I needed to marry Chloé instead of the other way around.

Grandpa might think Chloé was one of those fake fiancés he'd warned me about. But once he got to know her, got to see us together, he'd see that we were meant to be.

I thought about calling him. To tell him about her and that we were engaged. I glanced at the time. It was an hour later in Houston. And since he hadn't answered my text about the book, I decided he must be asleep already.

Grandpa had found his true love and, from the stories I'd been told, he hadn't hesitated to marry her. I think he just wanted that same happiness for me and he could see that I wasn't moving in that direction anytime soon.

The fact that I had never brought a girl home to the family dinners on Sunday was telling in and of itself.

Since it was too late to call Grandpa, I thought about calling my sister, Brooklyn. But I just as quickly decided against it. She'd just give me a hard time. Would scoff and say that she didn't believe me. Leopards don't change their spots. That's what she would tell me.

But I believed that people could change. I'd learned that from Grandma Savannah.

I don't think I was changing so much as I was redirecting my energy. I would put all the energy I had put into dating women in different cities into my relationship with Chloé.

We would have a good life.

Since I couldn't think of anyone I wanted to call, I picked up my iPad and started to read again.

Then I laughed at myself.

I should be talking to Chloé. She was right next door.

I wanted to shout it to the rooftops that I was engaged to her, but if I had any sense, I would be with her right now.

I got up, pulled on my jeans, and went to the door connecting our rooms.

I knocked lightly.

No answer.

She could be asleep.

But I'd left her less than an hour ago. Surely she wasn't asleep already.

I dialed the number downstairs and asked Peter to ring her room. I listened to the phone ringing through the door, but no one answered.

She could be in the shower.

There were so many reasons she didn't answer her phone... or her door.

But now I was worried.

I disconnected the phone and pressed my ear to the door. No sounds of anyone moving around. There was no way anyone could possibly sleep through that landline ringing like that.

In a bold move, I tried the door. The knob turned in my hand. I hadn't checked it when we got here. I had just assumed that it would be locked.

As a pilot, I had stayed in hundreds of hotel rooms and never, not once, had the connecting door been unlocked. But this one was.

I knocked again on the connecting door to her room. The door had been painted blue. I don't know why that stood out for me, but it did.

Since the door was unlocked, I slowly pushed it open, just a crack. I stopped and called her name.

Worried now, I pushed the door open and stood inside Chloé's room.

She wasn't here.

I had dropped her off, left her safely in her room, and went to my own room.

In the irony of it all, she had gone out.

CHAPTER 37
Chloé

I SAT in the back of an Uber and watched the trees race by in the darkness.

Finding an Uber in Whiskey Springs in the middle of the night had not been easy. I was fairly certain that I had paid double what it should have cost me.

Technically, I shouldn't have paid anything. Technically I should have waited for morning and taken one of the private jets back to Houston.

But I had to get away.

I had to get away from Mason. Just for a little while.

I liked him and was probably even falling for him, but I could not let him talk me into marrying him.

I was not of his world and I could not in good conscience allow this thing we had to continue.

And it wasn't just that. It was the whole thing with his grandfather. Mason wanted that Phenom his grandfather had promised him. If he got married.

So Mason had found me. Unsuspecting and willing.

I did not want to think about that too much.

The driver was quiet. A young man who didn't seem to

mind being pulled out to make a drive this time of night. He probably didn't mind the money that went with it either.

He played the news, the volume low, in the front of the car.

Using my phone, I went online and made a reservation for a hotel near the airport. In the morning, I would book a flight to Pittsburgh.

In the morning I would send Quinn a message telling him I was taking some personal time. Not the best way to start a new job. But I could use that as an excuse. Tell him I had some loose ends to tie up.

I wasn't quitting my job at Skye Travels. Not yet anyway. I had time—was taking time—to make that decision. But I had to be away from Mason in order to do it.

He clouded my judgement with his good looks and cerulean blue eyes. How was a girl supposed to think straight with him giving her his undivided attention? Of all the nerve.

I caught snippets of the news. The unemployment rate was up. Banks were struggling. Everything was about as normal as it could get.

I should be thankful to have the job I had. The pay was certainly better than the pay I'd been making in Pittsburgh.

I was probably being silly, even thinking about going back there. I had family there and I would see them during the holidays.

The thought brought a smile to my lips. Unless Mason had anything to say about it. If Mason had his way, we'd be spending much of our holiday in Whiskey Springs and probably the rest of it with his huge family.

Ava and I had tried to figure out just how big the Worthington family was, but we gave up. There were lots of Worthingtons. That was our scientific conclusion.

And from what I had been told, they were all close. Noah, the founder and owner, and his wife had the family—anyone who happened to be available—over at their house every Sunday.

Coming from the small family that I did, I could not even imagine what that must be like.

"We're an hour out, ma'am," the driver said.

Ma'am. Geez. I leaned back against the seat and closed my eyes.

Just what I needed. A reminder that I was nearing twenty-seven years old.

Twenty-seven and I was running away from the one marriage prospect I had at the moment.

Maybe I was an idiot.

Well. It was too late now.

I was an hour outside of Denver. Almost halfway. I had a hotel reservation. In the morning I would be on a flight to Pittsburgh.

And then I could think.

Right now I couldn't think.

I was still too close in proximity to Mason.

It certainly did not help that I kept replaying his kisses over and over.

But the further we got from Whiskey Springs, the more I felt sick to my stomach.

There was definitely something wrong with me.

CHAPTER 38
Mason

I LOOKED EVERYWHERE FOR CHLOÉ.

She was not in the saloon and she was not in any of the bars still open on Main Street. I had checked. Just in case.

It didn't take long to check every place that was open in the little town.

The thought of her out there somewhere made me feel sick.

Whiskey Springs might seem like a safe, sleepy little town, but there was danger everywhere.

After exhausting all the places she could possibly be, I went back into the saloon and stopped to talk to Peter again.

"She didn't come back?" I asked.

"No sir," he said, not looking me in the eye.

I hadn't known Peter very long, but I did know that he always made good eye contact.

"But you heard from her," I said.

Peter took a deep breath, looked over his shoulder at the empty bar, and met my gaze.

"Not exactly."

"What do you mean not exactly?"

"I promised her I wouldn't tell."

"Look, Man, I'm worried sick about her."

Peter wasn't budging.

"Did she tell you we're engaged?"

That seemed to shake Peter up a bit. "No." He ran a hand through his hair. "Okay. She's on her way to Denver."

"What?" I sat down on the nearest barstool.

"Why?"

"She didn't tell me why." Peter pulled a white cloth out of his belt loop and wiped the top of the already spotless counter. "My nephew drives people into Denver sometimes. I put her in touch with him."

"Your nephew."

I could not believe this.

All this time, Peter had known where Chloé was. In fact, he had helped set the whole thing up.

"Give me his number," I said.

Peter looked at me sideways.

"I just want to make sure she's safe."

"Don't you have her phone number?"

"It's a long story," I said.

"Dude," Peter said. "Always get their cell phone numbers. Especially if you're going to get engaged to them. Helps solve problems down the road."

I almost laughed as I pulled a business card out of my pocket. Peter had no doubt seen everything.

"Ask him to please call me. I promise I'm not a stalker."

"Didn't think you were," Peter said. He didn't say the words, but I knew what he was thinking. It would have been better if he'd just come right and said. "Don't cross that line."

If Chloé did not want to be with me, I would respect that.

But if she was merely scared about me proposing marriage, I could fix it.

I knew I'd moved too fast.

I blamed it on the people in the restaurant. They had caused this. I would have taken my time. Would have given her at least a couple of weeks before I actually proposed. It just seemed like the right thing to do.

"I'll tell him." Peter said, taking my card and sliding it into his pocket.

Peter would be in no rush.

I just had to trust him.

With my heart hurting, I went upstairs. I should get some sleep.

But no matter how much I knew I should get some sleep, I knew that it wasn't going to happen. Not tonight.

CHAPTER 39

Chloé

WHEN I WOKE the next morning, for just a fraction of a second, I had that wonderful sense of well-being that only comes from waking up.

That fraction of a second was followed by the confusion of not knowing where I was.

And then the last third fraction of that same second brought back the sick feeling that I had made a mistake.

I was in a hotel near the Denver Airport.

I didn't have a ticket for Pittsburgh, but my plan was to get one.

Surely a person could walk up to the counter at the airport and buy a ticket. I'd never tried.

Now that I had made my decision, I didn't want to think about how much more convenient it would have been to fly on one of the private planes I worked on.

It was funny. I knew those airplanes inside and out, yet I had to fly commercial.

I took a quick shower and dressed in a pair of jeans and shirt that I had in my travel bag. I took my time drying my hair. It had become a habit over the last week or so for me to spend a little more time on my appearance. It wasn't a bad habit to have. At least that was what Ava had been telling me for ages.

She would be pleased that I had finally listened. Even if it had nothing to do with her.

It had everything to do with Mason Johnson.

The guy—a pilot—had turned my life upside down. It was exactly why I did not date pilots.

They were trouble from the get-go.

I knew better.

But I was not dating him.

He had found me.

He had asked me to marry him.

I smeared on some soft red lipstick.

And yes, I had said yes, but that was rather beside the point.

The point of the matter was that he had disrupted my life.

Yes. I wanted to marry him. When I had agreed, I had agreed with all my heart.

However. Because I wanted to marry him, I couldn't.

It was really for the good of both of us.

I didn't need to become someone I wasn't and he didn't need to wake up in a week or a month or five years to discover that he had not married a socialite like he was supposed to.

We all had our places in society and mine was working on airplanes.

His role was to fly them.

He wanted to teach me to fly, but that would be upsetting the ecosystem.

I was not a pilot. If I'd wanted to be, I could have done that a long time ago.

I had a good career. A really good career. I was good at what I did.

Being good at what I did meant I should do it, right? My grandmother had told me that if a person had a gift for something, they should do it. Otherwise they were wasting the talent God had giving them.

I put on my pink leather jacket, gathered up my things, and headed out.

I took the shuttle to the airport. After I waited for an hour for it to finally get to the hotel, it took forever and made half a dozen stops before finally stopping at the terminal gate.

There were so many miserable people riding the shuttle. Angry people. People who looked like they were beaten down by the system.

By the time I got off the shuttle at my stop, I was feeling miserable myself. Just being around miserable people could make someone unhappy.

It didn't help that deep down—maybe not even all that deep —I really didn't want to be here.

I wanted to be back in Whiskey Springs with Mason. If I had stayed, we'd have gone to breakfast. Walked around town some more. I actually had blue jeans to wear like a normal person and not my flight suit.

Then we'd fly back to Houston. It would have been interesting to fly with Mason as the pilot. I had no doubt that he'd let me sit in the copilot's seat. Maybe I wouldn't even be nervous during takeoff with him at the controls.

But that was a fantasy world.

This was my real world.

I couldn't allow myself to get too used to having my luggage or overnight bag over whatever I happened to have with me delivered to my hotel room without even asking.

I was still baffled by that concept. I had forgotten that I'd left it at the airport, but if I remembered it I would have fully expected to have to drive back out to the airport to get my things. I'd actually been deep in the process of figuring out exactly how I would do that when I saw my bag sitting on the bed.

At any rate, I got in line to the ticket counter.

Looked like I was going to be here for a few hours. It was almost noon and I had made no progress to speak of in my journey back to Pittsburgh.

Maybe it wasn't meant to be. I shoved the thought away.

Not exactly how I wanted to spend my morning. My stomach was grumbling and I needed coffee. If Mason were here, he'd make sure we had both coffee and something to eat. He was good like that.

When I finally made it to the ticket counter and handed over my driver's license, the clerk scanned my information, then frowned.

"You already have a ticket," she said, looking at me with an odd expression—halfway between suspicion and disbelief.

"I don't understand," I said.

She slid my driver's license back across the counter.

"You're at the wrong terminal," she said.

I shook my head. "I just need—"

"Your terminal is at the end of the hall. Just show your identification to the guard at the door."

The guard at the door.

What had I done? Was I in some kind of trouble?

I didn't bother asking the clerk. She was finished with me and had moved on to the next customer.

I hoisted my travel bag back onto my shoulder. If I'd known I was going to be doing all this, I would have brought a rolling bag.

I would never leave home without a rolling bag again. Lesson learned.

I didn't see another terminal in the direction she had pointed, but I did see a guard, looking quite bored, sitting there behind a computer.

"I'm a little lost," I said.

"License."

I handed over my license. He studied it. Studied me.

"Took the long way around?" he asked, obviously not expecting an answer.

"I guess," I said.

"Just go through that door there," he said. "You'll end up where you need to be."

Quite confused, I went through the door he indicated, walked down a little hallway. I expected police to jump out at any time and arrest me for some crime I could not even imagine I might have committed.

People got wrongly accused of things all the time.

Maybe it was my name. Maybe there was someone else out there with my name, putting me on the blacklist.

I should have stayed in Whiskey Springs. This was one of the stupidest things I had ever done.

But no one jumped out at me.

And I made it to the next door without incident.

I stepped into a big open lobby with soft music playing in the background.

It looked like an officer's club, or how I imagined one to look. I'd never been in one, but I knew about them.

There were only a few other people here, one woman and three men, all sitting separately in their own private booths, all wearing business clothing.

I was going to have to do something about my wardrobe. My jeans were about as out of place in here as my flight suit would have been. Maybe even more so.

Drawn to the designer coffee kiosk, I was about to try to figure out how to make myself coffee, when a barista appeared from somewhere and asked what I would like.

"Vanilla latte, please," I said.

"One vanilla latte coming right up," she said. "Would you like a fresh blueberry scone to go with it?"

"Sure," I said, digging in my handbag for my credit card.

She noticed what I was doing. "You don't pay here," she said.

"Oh. Okay." I glanced around. "Where do I pay?"

"You paid when you bought your ticket. Here's your coffee," she said. "Have a seat and I'll bring your scone right out."

Utterly confused now, I took my coffee to an unoccupied sofa in a little private booth and sat down.

The coffee was wonderful. No doubts about that. This was no maintenance shop motor oil coffee.

The barista seemed to think I had a ticket. Well, they would soon find out that, not only did I not have a ticket, I was not a member of this club.

I hadn't even told anyone where I was going.

Maybe I had fallen down a rabbit hole.

Perhaps I could at least finish my coffee before they figured it out and escorted me out of here.

The barista brought a plate with a blueberry scone. "I brought you a muffin, too," she said. "'thought you might like a choice."

"Thank you." I wanted to ask her for more information but I didn't know what to ask.

I should be able to figure this out without coming across as completely ignorant. The reputation of all aviation engineers was riding on my back.

I tried both the scone and the muffin and since I couldn't decide which one I liked better, I ate both of them.

It occurred to me as I took my time eating in my private little booth, that I really did need to see about buying a ticket. As nice as it was here, I couldn't stay here all day.

It was almost like I'd stepped into an alternate reality.

One that was compelling enough that I didn't want to leave.

The barista appeared to take away my tray and empty. "I brought you a fresh coffee," she said. "If you'd like to trade with me."

It took me a moment to figure out that she wanted to take my coffee away, but she was giving me a fresh one.

I took the fresh coffee she offered and sat back in the booth.

A uniformed attendant holding a clipboard approached me.

I tensed. They had found out about me. This was it. I was about to be escorted out.

"Ms. Chloé Lewis?"

"Yes," I said, steeling myself for the worst. But I had not done anything wrong. It was just a mistake.

"Your flight is delayed."

She handed me something and smiled.

"I don't—"

"Since your flight is delayed, you have time for lunch. I'll be back in a few minutes to take your order."

I glanced down. A menu. She'd handed me a menu.

As I watched the woman walk away, I forced myself to close my mouth.

CHAPTER 40
Mason

Earlier that morning

I STOOD at the Whiskey Springs airport outside the terminal. I stood perfectly still.

The sun, just coming up, not even over the horizon yet, painted the sky, stretching endlessly beyond the snow capped mountains in a gold ombre hue. Dark gold at the horizon, fading to a light gold as it blended upwards.

It was a beautiful sunrise. As beautiful as any I had seen. Perhaps it was a harbinger of a good day.

The early morning breeze coming off the mountains carried a chill with it. There was snow in the forecast. None of the locals seems to mind springtime snow.

Black birds hopped on the ground, around me looking for food. A chipmunk ran up to me, stood on his hind legs. "Sorry. I don't have anything," I told him.

The chipmunk scurried off. People must be feeding them or they wouldn't do that.

The only sound was the rustle of the aspen leaves as the wind rushed through them.

I stood still because I felt like if I dared to moved, I would shatter into pieces.

Peter's nephew, the driver, had not called me. And since Peter was not at the saloon this morning, I couldn't ask him about Chloé.

I'd checked her room again. Just in case. But she wasn't there, of course. Last night Peter had said she was on her way to Denver.

It was Uncle Quinn who had called me this morning, waking me out a restless sleep.

I replayed the conversation in my head.

"What's going on with Chloé?"

"What do you mean?"

"I got a call from Peter. He said Chloé took off in the middle of the night."

"He told me that, too," I said, trying to figure out why Peter would call Uncle Quinn.

"He also told me you two are engaged." I wasn't sure if that was a question or a statement. I couldn't tell.

"Yes," I said. "But—"

"We need to fix this," he said. "Go to the airport and wait."

"I can take the Cessna." I was trying to catch up with what Uncle Quinn was talking about. I wasn't doing a very good job.

"Don't do that," Uncle Quinn said. That was definitely not a question.

"Why do you want me to go to the airport? I don't under—"

"Go to the airport. Wait. I'll be back in touch."

He disconnected the line.

I'd stared at my phone.

And now standing here at the airport, I knew nothing more than I had when I spoke with Uncle Quinn before dawn.

I stared at the sky until my eyes hurt. The only reason Uncle

Quinn would have me come to the airport was because he wanted me to fly.

Or maybe Uncle Jackson was coming out to fly me back to Houston. I had not seen him since he had landed with Chloé. Yesterday. Was it just yesterday? A lot had happened in less than a day.

In a single day, I had fallen even more in love with the girl of my dreams and gotten engaged.

I took a deep breath and since I didn't shatter, I stuck my hands in my pockets and gave up on trying to figure out what was going on.

Then I heard it. Just a faint sound. An airplane coming this way.

I searched the sky until I saw it.

I watched until the little jet came into view, circled the airport and came in for a smooth as silk landing.

My heart clenched as I realized it was a Phenom.

And as the pilot taxied along the runway, I saw that it wasn't just any Phenom, it was *my* Phenom 100. I knew because I recognized the fresh paint branding it as a Skye Travels airplane. That and this was the only Phenom 100 that Skye Travels owned. All the other Phenoms were bigger.

I waited as the pilot stopped the plane and went through the post flight checklist.

Then the door opened, the steps went down, and the pilot stepped down.

I blinked.

Grandpa?

"Come on," Grandpa said. "Don't just stand there."

Jarred out of my inertia, I strode to the plane.

"Why are you here?"

Grandpa removed his shades and smiled at me.

"I had a Phenom to deliver."

I shook my head. "I don't understand."

"You will," he said. "I have a meeting in town. You take the Phenom."

"Take it where?"

"Denver," he said. "The flight path is already entered."

I didn't move. I couldn't. My feet were frozen.

"How will you get home?"

"I'll take the Cessna. Go one," he said. "It's your airplane now. Take it for a spin."

"Mine?"

"Happy birthday, Grandson."

"But?"

"All you needed was some direction to put you on the right path. You're there now. All you have to do now is convince that girl of yours that it's her you want. Not this airplane."

CHAPTER 41
Chloé

"Miss Lewis. Your plane is here."

I uncurled my feet from beneath me and put them on the floor. A young man I hadn't seen before, wearing a uniform, stood in front of me. He smiled.

"May I take your bag?"

I nodded. I'd been close to falling asleep.

It was almost eleven thirty and the other passengers who had been waiting had gone, replaced by others.

I'd wandered around some while I waited on my lunch—everything made to order—and figured out that I was at a private terminal.

I didn't know why and no one would tell me why.

So I waited. I'm sure I could have walked out, but where would I go. I'd tried to buy a ticket, but they wouldn't sell me one.

So now, finally, I was about to find out what was going on.

I followed the attendant to the door leading out to the tarmac.

I missed a step when I saw the Skye Travels Phenom 100 sitting there, the door open, the steps down.

Then I saw Mason standing near the tail of the plane. He walked forward, one hand behind his back.

"Hi," he said.

"Hi." My greeting sounded like a question to my own ears.

"I heard you needed a ride," he said.

"Well, I didn't, but they wouldn't let me buy a ticket."

"You had one," he said.

"So they said."

He took a step forward.

Pulled a long-stemmed red rose from behind his back and held it out to me.

I took it from him and held it close in both hands. It smelled fresh, the petals had a little dew on them.

"Where can I take you?" he asked.

"I was going to Pittsburgh," I said. "To..." I could hard remember why I had started this trip.

"I can get you there."

"The Phenom," I said. "I thought..."

"It's mine now."

"But you're not—" married.

"Grandpa Noah decided I don't need to wait."

"Then... it's yours?"

"Well. It belongs to Skye Travels, but it's assigned to me. That's how it works."

"That's good," I said. "That means you don't have to get married." I tried to keep my voice even. To keep my bottom from trembling.

This meant Mason had no reason to get married. If he had the Phenom, he didn't have to get married.

"You don't have to—" My voice broke. I couldn't do this.

"Come here," Mason said, taking two steps to close the distance between us.

He wrapped me in his arms and, cupping the back of my

head, pressed my cheek against his chest. He rested his cheek against the top of my head.

"I don't have to get married now," he said.

I nodded. I knew that. And I should be happy. I didn't want Mason to marry me just to meet a requirement his grandfather set so he could get an airplane.

This was good. I took a ragged breath. I should be happy. For him. For me.

"I don't have to get married," he said again, "but I want to."

I stopped breathing. I just stood there, listening to my heart pound and my blood race through my ears.

"I want to marry you Chloé. I've known it since the first time I saw you."

I pulled back just enough to look up into his cerulean blue eyes.

He reached down and picked me up. Kissed me on the cheek.

"I've known I wanted to marry you Chloé Lewis since I first saw you."

"At the party?" I asked. My heart was so full, I thought it might burst with joy.

"In your red dress, yes," he said. "But before that."

I held on to him as he turned in a circle.

"When I met you underneath the airplane."

Underneath the airplane.

The fortune teller had gotten it right all those years ago.

"I sort of knew before that."

"How's that?" he asked.

"It's nothing. Just... maybe I'll tell you one day."

Maybe I would tell him that I had known since I was fourteen years old that I was going to meet my soulmate underneath an airplane.

Or maybe not.

We had the rest of our lives to figure these things out.

Epilogue

Chloé

December

The Phenom was ready to go. I'd checked the mechanical stuff myself.

Mason ran through the preflight checklist. Spoke something I couldn't understand into his microphone, then made a slight adjustment on the dash I didn't understand.

He looked over and grinned at me.

My heart skittered like it did anytime he looked at me.

I smiled back.

The diamond ring on my left ring finger caught the glint of the afternoon sunlight as we taxied along the runway.

"You ready?" he asked me.

I nodded.

The roar of the engines was loud. I didn't like wearing the headphones because it made me feel like I was in a tunnel.

Mason stopped the plane and sat waiting for our turn to take off.

We were on our way to Whiskey Springs for their Christmas festival.

We had a reservation—very hard to get this time of year—at the Whiskey Springs Saloon. One room. Registered and Mr. and Mrs. Mason Johnson.

I'd taken his name in a heartbeat.

If our track record was any indication, we'd be starting a family soon and I didn't like the idea of having children confused about what their name was going to be.

"Cleared," Mason said.

My heart did a little skip. It always did. But somehow over the course of the past few months, taking off had become my favorite part of flying.

I think it happened on a Sunday afternoon when Mason had given me the controls and I had taken the Phenom into the air.

We were probably breaking all kinds of aviation rules, but Mason did not worry. He just did what he thought was right. And that day he had thought I needed to take the airplane into the air.

The plane left the ground, nothing but air under it. Then we quickly gained altitude.

It wouldn't take long to get to Whiskey Springs. One thing I had quickly learned was that the Worthingtons jumped into an airplane to go somewhere like most people jumped into their cars. They were the wave of the future. Someday, far into the future, lots of people would fly like that.

I was wearing my red dress, the one I'd worn to the party that first night I'd officially met Mason. I had lots of fancy dresses now. It was what I wore when we flew. Or when we went out to dinner. Or to a musical or play.

I still had my office and I still worked my supervisor job. In the Worthington family, everyone worked. I still wore my flight suit on occasion, but as Mason's wife, no one questioned me anymore. If I donned a flight suit, it had to be serious.

After we quickly reached ten thousand feet, Mason turned to me.

"Do you want to drive?"

"No," I said. "You drive today."

I didn't tell him, but I loved seeing him in the cockpit, piloting the plane.

I wouldn't say that I had a thing for pilots now, but I would say that I had a thing for *a* pilot.

Mason locked in the autopilot and we cruised at ten thousand feet. I looked down at the highway winding below. The plots of farmland. The occasional house.

I was content. Happier than I could ever imagine I could have been.

"What are you thinking about?" Mason asked.

"Thinking how lucky I am."

"If you're lucky, just think how lucky I am. I got the prettiest girl at the ball."

"We both win," I said. "and everyone gets a prize."

"Have you been snooping in your presents?"

"I get presents?"

He looked at me sideways. "You know you do."

I did know. But I also knew that I didn't need presents.

I had the best present possible. I had Mason.

And that was all I wanted.

Keep Reading for a preview of
ON THE EDGE OF CHANCE...

BESTSELLING AUTHOR

KATHRYN KALEIGH

On the

Edge of

CHANCE

THE WORTHINGTONS

Preview

ON THE EDGE OF CHANCE

Brooklyn Johnson

THE WEATHER in Houston was sunny and clear, not a cloud in the cerulean sky. A typical hot September day, temperatures bumping into the nineties.

The weather in Boston was cool and cloudy. We would be landing in Boston in approximately three hours and fifty minutes. An overnight trip for me.

Tomorrow I had a long day. A flight from Boston to Chicago. Then Chicago to Houston. But I would be back in my own apartment for the next three days after that.

The flight was crowded, every seat taken. Two hundred forty-two souls aboard including pilots and crew.

The coffee was brewed, ready to serve. The drink cart was ready the run through the coach section. Pretzels and peanuts.

First class passengers got four choices. Short ribs, rolls, and salad or tortellini and salad. Smoked salmon or a grain bowl. Personally, I preferred the tortellini with a side of tofu. Today's desert, all around, was a brownie with ice cream. Not bad for a four-hour commercial flight.

First class had sixteen passengers today. As for coach, I had just gotten back from a crosscheck of that section.

In row thirteen, a mother desperately tried to comfort her wailing infant.

In row three, three teenage boys slapped their hands together playing rock paper scissors.

In row twenty-three, a couple on their honeymoon seriously needed to get a room.

People who worked with me insisted that I had a super power.

I could remember everyone's seat and row number and something about them. It wasn't hard.

It actually felt like cheating, the way I did it. Row thirteen. Unlucky. Wailing infant. People would complain.

Row three. Three teens.

Row twenty-three. Well. It was hard to forget what I saw before I tossed a blanket over them. If I was any judge, the girl would be sleeping soundly for the duration of the flight.

"Prepare for takeoff."

The veteran pilot, Warren Adams, I'd flown with dozens of times, ran the words together so that they sounded like one word. Passengers would have no idea what he said.

I took my seat near the front of the jet and fastened my seatbelt. Warren was no-nonsense and expected his crew to be the same.

Friendly and efficient. That was our mission. And according to all accounts, I was the poster child.

"Hey," My friend and coworker, Lacy Montgomery, sat in the seat across from me and fastened her belt as the plane started moving.

"Hey." I said, with a smile.

"Did you see the guy in the fifth row?"

"The one with the beard?" I asked, wrinkling my nose.

"Oh. Right," she said. "I forgot. You don't like beards."

She was right. I had been raised around clean-shaven men. And since I came from a large family, that said a lot.

"I'm sure he's a perfectly nice guy," I said. "Why don't you ask him out?"

Lacy laughed. "You know me too well." Then she asked what she always asked. "If he has a friend, you want to come along?"

And I said what I always said. "I don't date passengers or pilots."

"You have too many rules," Lacy said, good-naturedly.

"Keeps me honest."

We stopped talking as the airplane left the ground, leaving nothing more than a pocket of air beneath us. The baby in row thirteen wailed louder, although how that was possible, I didn't really know.

"We're off," I said.

"You're lucky you have first class," Lacy said.

"I have confidence in your ability to take care of a crying baby."

Lacy rolled her eyes and unbuckled. "Wish me luck."

"Good luck," I said as Lacy headed toward coach.

I didn't leave my seat until the pilot gave the all clear signal.

I was like that. Rules were there for a reason, so unless I had a good reason to do otherwise, I followed them.

That gave me about another four minutes before I had to get to work. Whoever said first class was easier than coach had never worked first class. And today it was just me.

Two of the other flight attendants had called in sick, cutting us short. I didn't hold it against them. They were doing what they were told. Better that than bring something contagious onto a plane full of people.

And I secretly preferred to work my section alone. Even if it was a lot of work.

I was not afraid of hard work.

If there was nothing to do, I would find something.

That was how I had been raised.

The red light went off and I released my seatbelt.

Show time.

Chapter 2
Benjamin Gray

It was a beautiful day for flying. A typical Wednesday. Clear blue skies.

Kids were back in school. Families were no longer on vacation.

We sat on the tarmac longer than usual, or at least it felt like it. And then we taxied forever. Maybe we were just going to drive to Boston.

I stuck my headphones into my ears, mostly to block out the sounds of a crying baby back in coach. I turned on some Frank Sinatra and closed my eyes. I used the time to think about my current project.

Once we were in the air, I could get some work done.

I had gotten myself into a bind with a deadline.

But my philosophy was family first.

And since my sister was having her first baby, it seemed like that should most definitely come first.

I could catch up on the work. I had no doubt about that. I just had to be left alone long enough. Sometimes I secured a private jet to take me across the country just to have a few hours of peace. I did some of my best writing in the air.

But since I had not been able to secure a private flight, I was stuck here in first class.

I usually flew with the private company, Skye Travels, but they had been booked up for today. I usually reserved ahead of time, but my sister's baby decided to come unexpectedly early.

Seemed like no matter how many pilots Noah Worthington hired, it was never enough.

Their reputation was stellar and they stayed booked out at least two weeks.

"Prepare for takeoff," the pilot announced over the speakers.

I was not a nervous flyer, but I did prefer to know who my pilot was. No reason. It was something I had gotten used to.

Reaching under my seat, I pulled out my laptop bag and powered on my computer.

I had a good, firm outline of my latest mystery novel, so all I had to do was to write the first draft. Second drafts were always easier because I had more of the idea down on my computer.

I was still on chapter one.

I lowered the volume on my headphones and pulled up my outline. The roar of the plane blocked out most of the background noise so it didn't take me long to get focused.

The passenger—an elderly well-dressed woman—sitting next to me tapped me on the shoulder.

"What are you doing?" she asked. "Are you working?"

"Yes," I said, trying not to sound annoyed.

"Are you going to Boston for work?"

"Yes," I said again, with a tight, forced smile. Actually the true answer was no. I was headed to Boston to be with my sister as she gave birth to her first child, but I certainly did not want to tell the woman that.

Babies were one of those topics one did not dare bring up with women. It tapped into their subconscious and they wanted to know everything.

She asked me something else, but pretending not to hear, I pointed to my headphones and shook my head. "Work," I said.

That usually did the trick. It was kind of funny. If people thought I was "working," they respected my time. If they somehow found out I was writing a novel, they thought it was okay to talk to me. Like writing wasn't "real work."

So I never purposely told anyone I was an author.

My seatmate looked disappointed that I didn't want to strike up a conversation, but it was better to disappoint her now than after I had wasted two hours of writing time.

Out of the corner of my eyes, I watched one of the uniformed flight attendants stopping at each aisle, taking drink orders. We had to pick our food orders at the time of ticket purchase, so there was no need to be bothered by that. And the thing about first class was the flight attendants didn't bother us until we wanted to be bothered.

So I kept my head down and my focus on the words on my screen. I was making some progress when it came time for the meals.

Unfortunately, the woman sitting next to me ordered the short ribs.

The flight attendant was careful not to disturb me as she handed over the plate. Even so, I caught a good whiff of the meat. I had to close my eyes and think about kittens chasing butterflies in a field to keep from gagging.

As a vegetarian, the scent of the short rib was enough to send me over the edge.

I couldn't blame anyone other than myself. I was the one who had chosen an aisle seat. I did not like to be cramped in, even if the view was better inside.

Just another reason to fly private.

On a private jet, there were no seatmates who ordered meat or asked pesky questions. It was just me and my own little world in the sky.

The fasten seatbelt light came on. I kept my seatbelt on. No reason not to. I was just sitting here anyway.

The pilot must have had some warning about impending turbulence.

The plane dropped, probably two feet, causing a lot of frightened gasps.

If I could, I would have told them that turbulence wasn't really dangerous. That it was to be expected and we would get through it just fine.

But even with my headphones in my ears, it was hard to concentrate, so I pulled them out and closed my computer.

I rested my hands on the computer and waited for the commotion to die down.

Instead, we hit another pocket.

The woman sitting next to me, noticing that my computer was closed, decided that it was okay to talk to me.

"Oh dear," she said. "I can't eat right now. Do you want this?" She held her plate out to me.

I instinctively leaned back, but there was nowhere to go. "No," I said, with my best polite, tight smile designed to be a friendly discouragement from interaction.

"Are you sure? I hate for it to go to waste. I paid extra for it."

"I can't," I said. "I'm allergic."

"Oh." The woman removed her plate from my face and set it back on her tray. "I'll have the young lady come and get it."

"That's not necessary," I said. "or really sa—"

The woman pressed the button.

"safe."

Didn't she realize that the flight attendant had to get up to come and see what the problem was? She was probably, most likely, buckled in herself, as she should be.

"Do you think she heard?" the woman asked, pressing the button again.

"I don't think it rings," I said. "I think it just lights up."

The flight attendant, holding onto the backs of the seats made her way toward our row.

"What can I get you Mrs. Evette?" she asked.

Mrs. Evette, my seatmate, held up her plate. "Would you take this away." She lowered her voice to a stage whisper. "He's allergic."

Right now I was feeling allergic to people.

"Of course," the flight attendant said, taking the plate.

Just as she took the proffered plate, we hit another pocket of turbulence. It was almost like it was on cue.

The flight attendant held the plate close, and to avoid spilling the contents on me, she spilled it all over herself.

I looked up just as she looked at me.

She had the most beautiful green eyes I had ever seen. I would describe them as jade, like a mysterious mermaid haunting rocky shores. In that brief instant, I sensed happiness and positivity in a soul that ran deep.

As the plane dropped again, I instinctively reached out to keep her steady, breaking eye contact in the process.

Now that was smart. Now we both had short rib juice on us, though in all fairness, the flight attendant was the one who had taken the brunt.

It was all down the front of her uniform.

"Oh dear," my seatmate said.

The flight attendant smiled. She actually smiled.

"It's okay," she said. "Don't worry. I'll get this cleaned up."

I released my hold on her and she turned, taking the offending plate, practically empty now, with her. The food was on the floor in the aisle next to my seat.

Mrs. Evette pulled napkins out of somewhere and, leaning over me, attempted to begin cleaning up the mess on the arm of my seat.

"Please," I said, taking the napkins from her. "Let me do it."

Kleenex, the woman was using Kleenex and I was making an

even bigger mess with them, but the flight attendant was already back with a bucket and a rag. She had the mess cleaned up in no time flat.

She must do this a lot, I thought absently.

"I'm so sorry this happened," she said to me. "Can I get you anything?"

"No," I said. "Please. Sit. Until we get through this turbulence."

"I'll be back," she said and disappeared.

I leaned my head back and tried to breathe through my mouth. Was it really necessary for people to eat on airplanes? Couldn't they just wait until they got where they were going?

Maybe this was why I wrote murder mysteries. It was my way of getting rid of offending people. A socially acceptable way of turning them into a character and killing them off.

About twenty minutes later, with no more turbulence, the red light went off.

The flight attendant came back as promised.

She handed me a drink. A vodka martini, dirty.

"How did you know to bring this?" I asked. "That I like these?"

"It was on your profile," she said. She had changed her uniform. I didn't even want to think about how that might have happened. The little bathrooms, even in first class, were barely enough to stand in.

"Right. I suppose it was." I didn't remember putting that on anything when I bought the ticket. The questions they did ask were optional, but I answered them anyway, mostly out of curiosity.

On occasion I drank a vodka martini when I flew with Skye Travels, but rarely.

Their databases didn't connect. Did they?

"Would you like your tortellini now?" she asked, with that same pleasant smile.

"That would be nice. Thank you." I really didn't want it. I only wanted it because she offered it. Good thing she didn't offer me something with beef in it. I just might have taken it.

There were some rules a man had to break and right now vegetarianism seemed like one of those breakable rules.

Apparently, since I had what they called short ribs on my tie, I was going to be smelling it all the way to Boston. What was the difference in that and eating it, really?

A few minutes later, the flight attendant brought my plate, vegetarian tortellini, and set it on the tray in front of me.

"Thank you," I said.

"Oh that looks so good," Mrs. Evette said. "So much better than what I ordered."

I sighed. Then did what any gentleman would do.

I handed it over to her. "Please," I said. "Take mine."

"Oh no," Mrs. Evette said. "I couldn't possibly."

"Of course, you can," I said. "Remember," I tapped my computer. "I have work to do."

She took the plate from me and happily munched on it while I happily tapped away on my computer keys.

It was a match made in heaven.

Keep Reading ON THE EDGE OF CHANCE...

Kathryn Kaleigh writes sweet contemporary romance, time travel romance, and historical romance.

kathrynkaleigh.com

Milton Keynes UK
Ingram Content Group UK Ltd.
UKHW010727130923
428592UK00004B/221